Stand By Your Pastor

FLOYD D. CAREY

STAND BY
YOUR PASTOR

*God's Partnership Plan
for the Local Church*

Dedicated to my wonderful wife, **Winnie**, who has stood
by my side as the joy of my life.
To the **faithful and fruitful Pastors** and
local church members with whom I have been honored
to partner in more than 50 years of ministry.
To **Marcus V. Hand**, a penman par excellence,
Sharon Dunsmore, a skilled graphic designer,
and **Marla Wilson**, a committed secretary.

Book Editor: Marcus V. Hand
Copy Editors: Esther Metaxas
Elizabeth Hightower

Library of Congress Catalog Card Number: 2003113370
ISBN Number: 087148-136-7
Copyright © 2003 by Pathway Press
Cleveland, Tennessee 37311
Printed in the United States of America

Stand By Your Pastor

God's Partnership Plan for the Local Church

— My Personal Guide —

_____

— My Pastor —

_____

— My Church Staff/Leaders —

_____

_____

_____

_____

_____

_____

_____

Statements of Support _____

Dr. Carey has stood by my side here at the Metropolitan Church for 12 years. He has also taught and led the people to stand with me in worship, building programs, outreach and fellowship. His book, *Stand By Your Pastor*, will support Pastors, strengthen congregations, and bring the two together as co-workers in ministry.

Raymond F. Culpepper, Senior Pastor
Metropolitan, Birmingham, Al.

I distributed 1,000 copies of Dr. Carey's last book, *Praying For Your Pastor and Church,* to my prayer team and altar workers. It brought us closer together in vision and ministry. To achieve great things for God, a Pastor must have his people praying for him and standing by him. The contents of *Standing By Your Pastor* will help achieve both of these objectives.

Jim Bolen, Senior Pastor
Trinity Chapel, Power Springs, Ga.

Pastors of the 21st century face challenges that are new and different as they lead the church to be a formidable force in society. As the paradigm shift takes place to change the focus from the past to the future, churches are looking outward from the ministry of self to a ministry of commitment. A commitment to reach the poor, the outcast and the homeless calls for a partnership, with the people standing by their Pastor to accomplish God's mission for the local church.

Lane Sargent, Senior Pastor
Sumiton, Al.

Floyd Carey's book, *Stand By Your Pastor,* is long past due. There is a great need for guidance to bring the Pastor and his people closer together. The resources found in these pages are invaluable. I highly recommend that every Pastor and every church member take the time to study this team-building manual.

Gary W. Sears, Senior Pastor
Mt. Olive Church, Cleveland, Tenn.

A local church will be blessed and "made happy" by studying *Stand By Your Pastor*. Unity and trust will help build a strong church. This book stimulates renewal and commitment.

Allan Mathura, Senior Pastor
Peachtree City, Newman, Ga.

Assistants or helpers are common, but armorbearers are uncommon. Assistants assist, while armorbears protect. Assistants do their duty, but armorbearers help others do their duty. God did not choose the sons of Moses or Elijah to succeed them, but He chose the men who stood by their sides and poured water on their hands. This book teaches you how to be an armorbearer by standing by your Pastor as a partner in ministry.

Bryan Cutshall, Senior Pastor
Twin Rivers Worship Center, St. Louis, Mo.

Moses needed Aaron; David needed Jonathan; Paul needed Barnabas; Jesus Christ even needed Peter, James, and John. Pastors need partners in ministry. There is not a more pressing, important or valuable topic to address in the church today. Thank you, Pastor Carey and the Youth and Christian Department for *Stand By Your Pastor*.

Mark L. Walker, Senior Pastor
Mount Paran North, Atlanta, Ga.

The church is at a crossroads. We will retreat into a maintenance mode or we will accept the challenge to become the missional church Jesus envisioned. To do this requires a repositioning of the traditional clergy-laity dichotomy that is typical of the maintenance model. The missional church moves to a "one people, one ministry" idea: the Pastor and congregation move in sync. When this occurs, a dynamic is released that is not just theoretical. This book is about this tremendous practical implication. I hope it receives widespread distribution.

Mike Chapman, Senior Pastor
City Church, Chattanooga, Tenn.

It is certain that Dr. Carey has chosen to address a subject that has the capability of producing immeasurable results. The impact of my own ministry has been greatly enhanced by devoted partners who have stood by me. I attribute my success to their prayerful encouragement and sacrificial devotion.

Gerald McGinnis, Senior Pastor
Parkwest Church of God, Knoxville, Tenn.

Stand By Your Pastor is a book that will benefit every local church. In changing times filled with uncertainties, Dr. Carey's book will be an asset in strengthening relationships between the Pastor, church leadership, members and staff. Partnership is the framework for both harmony and church health.

Joe E. Edwards, Senior Pastor
The Church at Liberty Square
Cartersville, Ga.

In Acts 12:5, we hear perhaps the most profound statement of the church supporting its Pastor: "So Peter was kept in prison, but fervent prayer for him was persistently made to God by the church (members). An angel was dispatched and Peter was delivered." *Stand By Your Pastor* is a book about prayer and support that will strengthen a local church.

Tony Scott, Senior Pastor
Cathedral of Praise, Sylvania, Oh.

Floyd Carey has worked with our church as a consultant. The ideas and concepts in *Stand By Your Pastor* are practical and workable. They have proven successful at Heritage.

Harold Bowman, Senior Pastor
Heritage Community Church, Severn, Md.

Contents

How to Bring Out the Best in Your Pastor
A Picture of Church Members
How the Pastor Brings Out the Best in You
The Power of a Pledge to Be a Partner With Your Pastor
Think With the Pastor

Profiles of Different Church Members
Coming Together as God's Team
Church Member's Pastoral Creed
Bringing Out the Best in Other Church Members
Profiles of Different Pastors
The Pastor's Creed
The Pastor and the People in Agreement
How to Be a Difference-Maker Church Member

Understanding Your Pastor
Understanding My Nature in Christ
Praying for Your Pastor
How to Honor Your Pastor
How to Increase Your Pastor's Effectiveness
How to Keep Pastor's Sermons Stored in Your Memory
Understand the Elements of Laity and Pastoral Leadership
Understand God's Plan of Tithing and Giving
Understand God-Honoring Compensation for Your Pastor
When Your Pastor Leaves
When a New Pastor Arrives
When Your Pastor Retires
The Value of Pledges, Proclamations and Covenants
My Covenant Commitment With My Pastor

Stand By Your Pastor

— Introduction —

"The local church is the hope of the world," states Bill Hybels in his book *Courageous Leadership.*

I fully embrace this declaration. Jesus said, "I will build My church" (Matthew 16:18). The church is built on the credentials of Christ as the Son of God, and is made up of the "called-out" ones (Romans 8:30). God's plan is for the "called-out" ones and the divinely "called" Pastor (2 Timothy 1:9) to become partners in the ministry of the local church.

Partnership is the power force of the church—the Pastor and the people uniting as a team to fulfill the Great Commission and to share the Good News of abundant life in Christ. This is God's plan, and He blesses His plan when it is clearly understood and Scripturally observed.

There are more than 350,000 churches in America, millions of members, and thousands of Pastors. Every church matters to God! Every member matters to God! Every Pastor matters to God. He wants all three to be blessed, coordinated in mission and spiritually successful. And He has a plan, a model, to ensure this will happen.

The authentic model for church growth and health is the Master's Model. It is Motivated by Love (God's mercy), Measured by Values (Ministry of Christ), and Managed through Partnership (Holy Spirit, Pastor, and the people). This model produces results because it unifies all the forces of heaven with all the forces in the local church to perform kingdom ministry.

God wants you to stand by your Pastor, to become a co-worker with him. When you stand by your Pastor, you connect with his calling, bond with his burden (vision) and find an anchor in his anointing. It builds a solid foundation of trust. **TRUST** is the binding factor for strong, vibrant, growing churches. Trust brings the Pastor and people **T**ogether in spirit, establishes **R**espect for each other, **U**nites in purpose, **S**tabilizes in doctrine, and **T**rains for visionary service. *Good churches become great churches when members trust their Pastor and each other.*

The purpose of this book is to guide you in standing by your Pastor by building a "trust" relationship with him. It is a study course that will bring the entire church together to learn about God's plan for the Pastor and the people — what it means, where it leads, and what it achieves.

A brief overview of the five chapters will help prime your spirit for the flow of the study. Each chapter begins with a poem and the ABCs of the subject that will be discussed in the session. At the conclusion of each lesson there will be a pledge, a covenant, or a proclamation to be embraced or signed. There will also be questions to stimulate interaction. The material covers a step-by-step approach to standing by your Pastor.

Chapter One sets forth the premise for authority and leadership in the church—the holy calling of the Pastor and the Scriptural calling of members. Both are called of God and are given specific responsibilities in tending, feeding, and protecting the flock of God, and in seeking and finding the lost. The importance of core values in ministry is stressed.

Chapter Two points out the pressure on your Pastor's ministry. Often the expectations are unrealistic. You will be asked to complete an Awareness Quiz and a Personal Quiz to determine your understanding and support of your Pastor's ministry. The Five-Way Test will be something you can utilize to determine appropriate conduct or participation in church work.

Chapter Three focuses on God's plan of partnering with your Pastor in ministry. The Seven Laws of Partnering With Your Pastor offer a clear path to follow. Mistakes to avoid are listed and a blueprint on how to Build a Bridge to Your Pastor is given. An illustrative picture of a Pastor and a Church Member is uniquely set forth.

Chapter Four gives Seven Profiles of Different Church Members and Seven Profiles of Different Pastors. Regardless of styles or personalities, an Agreement Plan can bring everyone together. Steps to take in being A Difference-Maker Church Member are listed.

Chapter Five gives positive guidance on how to support your Pastor. It begins with understanding what makes him Tick, Click, Kick, and Stick. Forms are provided for you to map your Pastor's gifts and your personal gifts for ministry. Patterns, procedures, and methods of standing by your Pastor in prayer, church programs, and personal commitment are colorfully outlined.

Resource material follows Chapter Five. This material can be used in the church bulletin, Pastor Appreciation activities, Sunday school lessons, and church and Pastor programs. It will help maintain a focus and a priority on recognizing the position of the Pastor and the partnership of the congregation with him.

As you study the material it might appear that some subjects are covered more than once by using a different approach. The five chapters support each other, and it was necessary to continually emphasize the various avenues that partnership must travel in order to establish a clear vision and a strong platform for performance. I am pro-church, pro-member and pro-Pastor. I think my emphases come through in the text.

— Methods for Teaching the Material —

Stand By Your Pastor is designed to be used as a study course or for individual reading. The greatest impact for a local church will be a study course where interaction can take place. Here are some tips for using the book as a study course.

Make the study of *Stand By Your Pastor* a priority. Put it at the top of the church's "to do" list. It can make the difference between a God-pleasing church and a non-productive church.

Select a strong lay leader to teach the course to the congregation.

Determine a specific time: five Wednesday evenings, a Saturday morning seminar, a two-hour Sunday evening session, or a five-night "give it all" approach.

Encourage church members to purchase a personal copy of the book so they can underline key points, fill-in quizzes, and record information on the various forms.

Launch the study with a full base of prayer. Ask God to bring the church together to study His partnership plan and how it is the foundation for the future.

— Certificate of Partnership —

Each person who studies the course with a group, or who reads the book, will receive a recognition certificate—**Partner With My Pastor In Ministry**. This attractive certificate, suitable for framing, will designate you as a church member actively involved in church ministry and supporting God's plan for the local church. This book is part of the AIM/CTC program. For information and certificates contact: *Church of God Department of Youth and Christian Education*, P.O. Box 2430, Cleveland, TN 37311-2430.

— Commendation for Vision —

Thank you for embracing the vision with me of God's plan of the Pastor and the people as partners in the ministry of the local church. I do believe "the hope of the world is the local church." I also believe that as we embrace God's partnership plan the church will experience solid, stable, mounting influence, and numerical growth. May your life be impacted as you study *Stand By Your Pastor.*

— My Prayer for You —

Lord of boundless love, thank You for Your plan of the Pastor and the people serving You as partners in ministry. May this study course create a clearer vision, a deeper respect and stronger commitment to this partnership. Through Your investment in the church, it is the hope of the world. Together, we will proclaim Your cause with new insights for effectiveness, and with a new intensity to reach our full potential in Christ. Amen.

– Floyd D. Carey

CHAPTER ONE

The Position of Your Pastor

I WILL STAND BY MY PASTOR

I will stand by my Pastor,
Displaying strong spiritual pride,
As a partner in ministry,
Letting him know I'm by his side.

I will stand by my Pastor,
God's torch a light in my hand,
Serving as a gospel witness,
Revealing the wonders of His plan.

I will stand by my Pastor,
Like him, always on call,
Modeling the life of the Master,
Praying I will never fall.

I will stand by my Pastor,
Anchored in loyalty and trust,
Embracing his vision and dream,
We become one on God's team.

The ABCs of Recognizing the Position of Your Pastor

A - **ACCENTUATES** God's partnership plan for His church.

B - **BUILDS** character, maturity and Biblical credibility.

C - **CREATES** a positive, influential community image.

D - **DEVELOPS** teamwork in the mission of the church.

E - **ENGAGES** the entire church family in warm fellowship.

F - **FOSTERS** coordination in cultivating discipleship.

G - **GIVES** a compelling, friendly, exciting spiritual glow.

H - **HOLDS** the church together as a big, happy family.

I - **INSPIRES** openness and unity in praise and worship.

J - **JUMP-STARTS** initiative in spreading the Good News.

K - **KILLS** misunderstandings, division, discord and tension.

L - **LEADS** the congregation to exhibit the love of Christ.

M - **MOBILIZES** the skills and talents of the entire laity.

N - **NURTURES** wholeness and wellness in the church.

O - **OPENS** doors to influence community and civic leaders.

P - **PROMOTES** receptivity to Biblical teaching and training.

Q - **QUALIFIES** for power to be visionary and productive.

R - **REMOVES** obstacles that hinder excellence in ministry.

S - **STRENGTHENS** the church body for spiritual warfare.

T - **TRAINS** youth and involves them for future leadership.

U - **UNITES** leaders as they equip believers for ministry.

V - **VERIFIES** the meaning of Christian compassion and care.

W - **WORKS** as a witness of true, uplifting church harmony.

X - **EXPELS** attitudes that damage healthy church growth.

Y - **YOKES** believers together to achieve Kingdom tasks.

Z - **ZAPS** outside influences that try to destroy progress.

The Position of
Your Pastor

The role your Pastor plays is one of the most important in the Kingdom of God. He is a choice gift, a valuable treasure, God gives to the church.

> *He Himself gave some to be . . . pastors and teachers, for the equipping of the saints for the work of ministry, for the edifying of the body of Christ* (Ephesians 4:11, 12).

Your Pastor's call from God is the unshakable foundation for his ministry. Without God's call he would simply be an employee of the church—a spiritual CEO, gifted speaker, fund-raiser and a positive attitude motivator. In any of these capacities, he could do a good work and guide individuals in living a better life; however, *he would not be God's voice to the people.*

With the Lord's call he is God's representative to the people—to relay God's messages through the Word and through worship, to guide in paths of righteousness, to help shape in Christlikeness and to lead in expanding God's Kingdom on earth. *He is God's voice to the people.*

When the Pastor's call is fully understood in light of Holy Scripture and the will of God, the local church is blessed with all spiritual blessings. There is a continual reaping of the harvest of the unchurched in the community. Since church effectiveness and evangelism are based on believing in, and embracing, the Pastor's call from God, it is essential to look at the definition of his call as presented in the Bible.

Your Pastor's Call to the Ministry

Your Pastor's call to ministry is:

A Holy Call – "[God] has saved us and called us with a holy calling, not according to our works, but according to His own purpose and grace" (2 Timothy 1:9).

A Call of Divine Appointment – "I was appointed a preacher, an apostle, and a teacher" (2 Timothy 1:11).

A Call of Grace – "God . . . separated me from my mother's womb, and called me by His grace, to reveal His Son in me, that I might preach Him among the Gentiles" (Galatians 1:15, 16).

A Call to Unshakable Trust – "According to the glorious gospel of . . . God, which was committed to my trust" (1 Timothy 1:11, KJV).

A Call of Honor – "No man takes this honor to himself, but he who is called by God " (Hebrews 5:4).

A Call With Authority – "Even if I should boast somewhat more about our authority, which the Lord gave us for edification" (2 Corinthians 10:8).

A Call to Be a Torch – "[Jesus] makes His . . . ministers a flame of fire" (Hebrews 1:7).

A Call With Demands and Consequences – "If I preach the gospel, I have nothing to boast of, for necessity is laid upon me; yes, woe is me if I do not preach the gospel" (1 Corinthians 9:16).

A Call to Total Commitment – "Be watchful in all things, endure afflictions, do the work of an evangelist, fulfill your ministry" (2 Timothy 4:5).

A Call to Shepherd – "I will give you shepherds (Pastors) after my own heart, who will lead you with knowledge and understanding" (Jeremiah 3:15, *NIV*).

A Call to Be an Example – "Be an example to the believers in word, in conduct, in love, in spirit, in faith, in purity" (1 Timothy 4:12).

A Call to Instruct – "If you instruct the brethren in these things, you will be a good minister of Jesus Christ" (1 Timothy 4:6).

A Call Based on Faith – "I thank Christ Jesus our Lord . . . because He counted me faithful, putting me into the ministry" (1 Timothy 1:12).

A Call to Endure Infirmities – "I will not boast, except in my infirmities" (2 Corinthians 12:5).

A Call to Testify – "I consider my life worth nothing to me, if only I may finish the race and complete the task the Lord Jesus has given me — the task of testifying to the gospel of God's grace" (Acts 20:24, *NIV*).

Let me state again, your Pastor's call from God is the unshakable foundation for his ministry. His call gives him grace to stand, grit to endure, and gifts to minister effectively. His call enables him to accept all the responsibilities assigned to him. Consider the status of your Pastor:

Appointed . . .
To **Proclaim** good news
To **Lead** in worship
To **Equip** the saints
To **Shepherd** the sheep
To **Guide** in honoring God

Anointed . . .
To **Nurture** with love
To **Proclaim** with power
To **Lead** with reverence
To **Equip** with authority
To **Guide** with expectation

Commanded . . .
To **Love** the children
To **Train** the youth
To **Nurture** the adults
To **Marry** the young
To **Bury** the dead

Commissioned . . .
To **Provide** for the needy
To **Feed** the hungry
To **Care** for widows
To **Visit** the sick
To **Minister** to prisoners

The sense of a high and holy calling marks gifted Pastors and teachers. It is a divine calling from God Himself. Like Old Testament priests, Pastors are called to do a special work, and a mark of anointing crowns their ministry. They, too, are under orders. They are not free to do whatever they would like to do because they are accountable to God and must carry out His assignments.

New Testament writers continually said of themselves—and were recognized by others—that they were called, chosen and anointed. Your Pastor follows in the line of men of God who are called for a special work.

- Like Noah, your Pastor is called to announce judgment and to tell people how to escape it.
- Like Abraham, he is called to be a patriarch to those in his care.
- Like Moses, he is called to leadership.
- Like Samuel, he is called to anoint other leaders.
- Like Nehemiah, he is called to rebuild broken walls.
- Like David, he is called to provide God's people with joy and music.

- ◆ Like Peter, he is called to pastor God's sheep.
- ◆ Like John, he is called to communicate a new vision to God's people.
- ◆ Like Paul, he is called to teach, encourage, correct, exhort, admonish, and equip the church he is serving.

You, too, are called by God. It is important to understand this calling if you desire to stand by your Pastor in the way the Bible outlines.

- ◆ You are called out of darkness into God's marvelous light (1 Peter 2:9).
- ◆ You are called to belong to Jesus Christ (Romans 1:6).
- ◆ You are called according to God's purpose (Romans 8:28).
- ◆ You are called to be a saint (1 Corinthians 1:2).
- ◆ You are called into intimate fellowship with Jesus our Lord (1 Corinthians 9).
- ◆ You are called to live in peace (1 Corinthians 7:15).
- ◆ You are called to be free (Galatians 5:13).
- ◆ You are called to hope (Ephesians 1:18).
- ◆ You are called to bless people as well as to inherit a blessing (1 Peter 3:9).
- ◆ You are called to God's eternal glory (1 Peter 5:10).

What Makes a Pastor Effective

Listed below are seven qualities or principles that determine a Pastor's effectiveness. Rate the value of each item by placing a one by the most important, a two by the second most important, and so on down the line until you have included all seven points.

_____ Passion for God (calling)

_____ Partnership With the People

_____ Prayer and Appreciation Support

_____ People Skills

_____ Preaching That Connects

_____ Planning and Developing Disciples

_____ Promotional Enthusiasm

All the qualities and principles listed are of major importance. However, there are two points around which all the others orbit: *Passion for God* (calling) and *Partnership With the People*. Unless the people and the Pastor come together in love and respect, the ministry of the Pastor will be surface and short-lived.

> *I thank my God every time I remember you. In all my prayers for all of you, I always pray with joy because of your partnership in the gospel from the first day until now* (Philippians 1:3-5, *NIV*).

This quiz pinpoints the two essentials for effectiveness in a Pastor's ministry: his own call and the people's partnership with him in God's work. Often the expectations and opinions of the people are different from God's plan.

Therefore, it is important to look at two areas of impact in order to have a solid structure for ministry with your Pastor: *The Call and Character of a Pastor* and *God's Oversight of a Pastor's Ministry*.

The Call and Character of the Pastor

In 2 Timothy Paul gives the description of the call, character and challenges of a Pastor. The nature of his work calls for congregational understanding, prayer and support.

A Pastor, called and commissioned by God:

- ◆ Has "genuine faith" (1:5).
- ◆ Is gifted "of God" (1:6).
- ◆ Has the spirit "of power and of love and of a sound mind" (1:7).
- ◆ Is "not . . . ashamed of the testimony of our Lord" (1:8).
- ◆ Is "called . . . with a holy calling . . . according to [God's] own purpose and grace" (1:9).
- ◆ Is loyal to the faith and "hold[s] fast the pattern of sound words" (1:13).
- ◆ Is "strong in the grace that is in Christ Jesus" (2:1).
- ◆ Commits the message of God's love to faithful men "who will be able to teach others" (2:2).

- "Endure[s] hardship as a good soldier of Jesus Christ" (2:3).
- Competes in spiritual athletics "according to the rules" (2:5).
- Is a worker who is not "ashamed, rightly dividing the word of truth" (2:15).
- "Shun[s] profane and idle babblings" (2:16).
- Is "sanctified and useful for the Master, prepared for every good work" (2:21).
- "Flee[s] . . . lusts [and] pursue[s] righteousness, faith, love, peace . . . out of a pure heart" (2:22).
- "Avoid[s] foolish and ignorant disputes" (2: 23).
- Is "a servant of the Lord," does not quarrel, is gentle, able to teach, is patient, and "in humility correct[s] those who are in opposition" to God's stated plan (2:24, 25).
- Turns away from people who have "a form of godliness but [deny] its power" (3:5).
- "Carefully follow[s] [the] doctrine" of spiritual mentors (3:10).

God's Oversight of the Pastor's Ministry

God directs the ministry of your Pastor. This is not always understood by church members and often leads to behavior that is not Biblical. A Pastor's decisions are viewed differently when it is understood that he does not act on his own. He is under God's control and supervision. God outlines the paths he must walk. Research the following scriptures that indicate God's guidance:

God calls and assigns the Pastor's tasks.

Preach the Word! Be ready in season and out of season. Convince, rebuke, exhort, with all longsuffering and teaching (2 Timothy 4:2).

Then I will give you shepherds (Pastors) after my own heart, who will lead you with knowledge and understanding (Jeremiah 3:15, *NIV*).

God sets the boundaries of his ministry.

Now when they had gone through Phrygia and the region of Galatia, they were forbidden by the Holy Spirit to preach the word in Asia (Acts 16:6).

God gives him grace for ministry.
According to the grace of God which was given to me, as a wise master builder I have laid the foundation, and another builds on it. But let each one take heed how he builds on it (1 Corinthians 3:10).

God works in and through him to be a model.
But you, O man of God, flee these things and pursue righteousness, godliness, faith, love, patience, gentleness (1 Timothy 6:11).

God gives him assurance and confidence.
The Lord said, "I chose you to speak for me to the nations." I replied, "I'm not a good speaker, Lord, and I'm too young." "Don't say you're too young," the Lord answered, "If I tell you to go and speak to someone, then go!" (Jeremiah 1:4-7, *CEV*).

God charges the people to embrace their Pastor.
Be careful not to neglect the Levites (Pastors) as long as you live in your land (Deuteronomy 12:19, *NIV*).

God gives the Pastor grace to endure.
None of these things move me; nor do I count my life dear to myself, so that I may finish my race with joy, and the ministry which I received from the Lord Jesus, to testify to the gospel of the grace of God (Acts 20:24).

God opens and closes doors for him.
Meanwhile praying also for us, that God would open to us a door for the word, to speak the mystery of Christ, for which I am also in chains (Colossians 4:3).

God places equal value on all the ministries.
Neither he who plants is anything, nor he who waters, but God who gives the increase (1 Corinthians 3:7).

God outlines the theme of the Pastor's preaching.
For we do not preach ourselves, but Christ Jesus the Lord, and ourselves your bondservants for Jesus' sake (2 Corinthians 4:5).

A Spirit of Yieldedness

There must always be a spirit of yieldedness and openness to understanding God's purpose and responding to His ideal will. The basis for this understanding is to remember that He is in control of the church, its operation and the selection of its Pastor. We must depend on God's leadership in sending and supporting the Pastor. This story of a church looking for a suitable Pastor supports the fact that we cannot rely on our own wisdom or judgment.

- The first man the church interviewed was named Moses. When they found out he stuttered and occasionally lost his temper over trivial things, they marked him off their list.

- They interviewed someone named Abraham and found out that during a tough time, he ran away to Egypt. While there, he shaded the truth a little, and lied to cover up his deception. So they marked him off.

- They interviewed a musician/Pastor named David and found him very gifted but morally flawed. He was quickly rejected.

- Then the committee decided to interview a woman candidate. Esther was a beautiful woman, but you wouldn't want someone who once won a beauty contest as your Pastor.

- They interviewed a man named Hosea. He was turned down because his family life was in shambles, and his wife was a prostitute.

- They interviewed a man named Jeremiah, but he was too emotional. His reputation as an alarmist and a pain in the neck did him in with the committee.

- John the Baptist came before them, but he dressed—well, different, almost like a hippie. Who would feel comfortable with this nut cruising the crowd at a church supper?

- They interviewed someone named Peter, and found he had a bad temper and had once publicly denied the Lord.

- They talked to a really bright candidate named Paul, but he was the least tactful of all. His appearance was contemptible and his answers harsh at times. Plus, he had a reputation for preaching too long.

◆ They interviewed a woman named Lydia, but, because she was a successful businesswoman, they thought she would be too threatening to a lot of men. Besides, she wore too much purple.

◆ Timothy showed a lot of potential, but he was awfully young and was known to be on some questionable medicine.

◆ Finally, they interviewed one who seemed very practical, was good with money, cared for the poor and dressed well. They all agreed he would be a great candidate. His name was Judas.

What do the views of some people indicate? They reveal a lack of understanding of God's plan for the Pastor and the people to do the work of the church together. This is why I emphasize again that understanding the call and the character of your Pastor must be fully understood in order for the church to have God's approval and power.

Let's continue to outline God's hand on your Pastor and the three-fold ministry that God gives him:

◆ A Caring Shepherd
◆ A Faithful Soldier
◆ A Compassionate Servant-leader

Your Pastor Is a Caring Shepherd

The Lord Himself is the Great Shepherd. David understood this truth, and composed the 23rd Psalm as a song of praise to Him. Other scriptures celebrate this same truth:

In Psalm 80:1, the Lord is the Shepherd of Israel who leads Joseph like a flock.

In Isaiah 40:11, He feeds His flock like a shepherd, gathering the lambs in His arms and carrying them in His bosom.

In John 10:11, Jesus is the Good Shepherd.

In Hebrews 13:20, He is the Great Shepherd of the sheep.

In 1 Peter 2:25, He is the Shepherd and Overseer of our souls.

While Jesus is the Great Shepherd, Pastors are shepherds under Him. In the New Testament, the same Greek word is translated both *Pastor* and *shepherd*. Jesus used it in John 10:11, 14, where He said twice, "I am the good shepherd"; and Paul used it in Ephesians 4:11

where he said, "[God] Himself gave some to be . . . pastors." This is the only time the word *Pastor* is found in the New Testament, and one of only nine times in the entire Bible.

In 1 Corinthians 4:1, 2, spiritual leaders are *stewards*, or household managers who manage resources and assets for a household under the direction of the owner. Church leaders manage the resources that belong to God and disperse them to His church as stewards.

In 1 Timothy 2:7 (*NIV*), spiritual leaders are *heralds*. In a historical context they are town criers, proclaiming the king's message. In a contemporary context, we are broadcasters, disseminators, a vast internet spreading the Good News.

In 1 Timothy 2:7, spiritual leaders are *teachers*. To teach others what Jesus commanded is the responsibility of every believer (Matthew 28:18-20). But in 1 Peter 5:1-4, spiritual leaders are *shepherds* who have the responsibility to feed the flock of God and oversee it.

> *Remember your leaders, who spoke the word of God to you. Consider the outcome of their way of life and imitate their faith. Obey your leaders and submit to their authority. They keep watch over you as men who must give an account. Obey them so that their work will be a joy, not a burden, for that would be of no advantage to you* (Hebrews 13:7, 17, *NIV*).

The role and responsibilities of a shepherd are very demanding. The book, *Turnaround Churches*, makes this statement:

> *Shepherds of biblical times lived and worked in parched, inhospitable, and dangerous environs. The occupation was not for the weak. Shepherds encountered harsh weather, rough terrain, and predators . . . loneliness was expected. . . . Solitude was the norm. . . . Uncertainty was daily fare . . . The shepherd never heard a word of gratitude from those he carried, restored, fed, and protected. He, however, did not work for the sheep. He tended sheep for his master.*

Yes, the work of your Pastor-shepherd requires a clear vision, total commitment, and boundless energy. Consider the scope of his responsibilities as set forth in the characteristics of a shepherd:

Characteristics of a Shepherd

1. Administers healing to bruised and wounded sheep.
2. Carefully monitors the growth of the flock.
3. Creates a spirit of togetherness among the flock.
4. Designs new ways to keep the flock together.
5. Develops a spirit of adventure, happiness and contentment.
6. Directs the flock in sound doctrine.
7. Encourages the sheep to graze on higher ground.
8. Feeds the flock a balanced diet.
9. Gives each member of the flock personal attention.
10. Grooms and nurtures the flock.
11. Guards and protects the flock.
12. Helps the sheep stay healthy and vibrant.
13. Instructs in following paths of righteousness and peace.
14. Is faithful in his duties as a guardian.
15. Is known for sound speech.
16. Knows the best routes to clear and healthy water.
17. Knows the sheep of the flock, and calls them by name.
18. Leads the flock by day and night.
19. Protects and cares for young sheep.
20. Provides a variety of scenery for the flock.
21. Provides peace through assurance and safety.
22. Provides an atmosphere for contentment.
23. Reminds the flock of their responsibilities to reproduce.
24. Restores sheep who have fallen.
25. Searches for sheep who go astray.
26. Serves as a role model for the flock.
27. Sets a watch so sheep will not be influenced to leave the flock.
28. Shows each member of the flock how to contribute.
29. Shows the sheep how to remain clean and white.
30. Shows the way of faith and works.
31. Stays on watch for wolves teaching false doctrines.
32. Surrounds the flock with love that warms, defends, and edifies.
33. Teaches the flock God's code for conduct.

34. Tells each sheep his/her value and significance to the flock.
35. Trains sheep to lead other sheep.
36. Trains the flock to trust the Great Shepherd.
37. Warns of the dangers lurking in the woods near the pasture.

As a shepherd, your Pastor must follow the example of Christ who said, "I am the good shepherd." As a good shepherd under the Good Shepherd, your Pastor must give his total life to fulfilling His calling.

On the Shoulders of Your Shepherd

You have seen the picture of Christ, our chief Shepherd, carrying a lamb on His shoulders. This picture depicts His love for us, the sheep of His pasture, and His willingness to protect us, to provide for us, and to walk the path of life with us.

Christ has appointed your Pastor to be your earthly shepherd. He carries tremendous responsibilities on his shoulders in order to fulfill God's purposes for your life.

The weight of God's call is always on the shoulders of your Pastor. It is an irreversible call. It cannot be delayed, suspended, or set aside. It is divine in nature. The call is always on the shoulders of your shepherd—*heavy, demanding.*

The Duty to Equip

Your Pastor must live a holy life and perform Christ-inspired service. He must also equip the people of the church to live holy, and to engage in real life ministry that reflects the nature of Christ and that expands His Kingdom on earth. His equipping duties are always on his shoulders—*heavy, demanding.*

The Expectations of the People

In writing to the people he had pastored, Paul said, "So I am happy to give everything I have for you, even myself" (2 Corinthians 12:15, *NCV*). He worked with the people and for the people without limits. This is the nature of your Pastor. He is always working for you and for your spiritual health. He is always ready, available, on duty—

preaching, training, and encouraging. The needs and expectations of the people are always on his shoulders—*heavy, demanding.*

The Daily Flow of Faith

The duties of your Pastor never let up. He must always be in touch with God to receive instructions from His Word to guide you. It is a daily, hourly assignment. There must always be a flow of faith to intercede for the people, to instruct the people, and to inspire the people. The need and cost of a daily flow of faith is always on the shoulders of your Pastor—*heavy, demanding.*

Actually, you are on the shoulders of your Pastor. He carries you so you can develop into a mature, motivated, ministering believer. Now we will look at four ways you can help your Pastor carry the weight that is on his shoulders.

1. **Look Up and Offer Up**
   Look up to God in daily prayer for your Pastor. Offer up thanksgiving for his ministry. Ask God to protect him, lead him, and bless him—richly, abundantly.

2. **Stand Up and Speak Up**
   Stand up for the ministry of your Pastor; stand by his side. Speak up about his goals, plans, and dreams and champion the people to back them—richly, abundantly.

3. **Hook Up and Wake Up**
   Hook up with your Pastor in a specific ministry. Wake up to the great potential of the local church to be a lighthouse to the lost—guiding, loving, leading. Be dependable, accountable, honorable—richly, abundantly.

4. **Lift Up and Talk Up**
   Lift up the banner of togetherness in the local church. Talk up the benefits of unity and harmony in working with the Pastor, with church leaders, and with each other — richly, abundantly.

"So, affectionately longing for you, we were well pleased to impart to you not only the gospel of God, but also our own lives, because you had become dear to us" (1 Thessalonians 2:8).

To stand by your Pastor, you must assist him in shepherding the local church. In Acts 20:28, Paul told the leaders of the Ephesus church: "Be shepherds of the church of God, which he bought with his own blood" (*NIV*). To boil down the ministry of your Pastor/shepherd, four functions are dominant: Tend the flock of God; Feed the people of God; Protect the church of God; and Seek the lost.

You can be a coworker, a great supporter and contributor, in all four of these areas.

Your Pastor Is a Faithful Soldier

Your Pastor is a soldier in the army of the Lord. He is always on active duty; he is never on leave. It is necessary for him to be fully armed and vigilant. The battle he fights is not a picnic. It is not a holiday excursion. Instead, it is spiritual warfare. And to effectively wage war against the many spiritual enemies he faces, your Pastor needs for you to be active in God's army, too. This is not a time for carelessness, boastfulness and underestimating the enemy. To be guilty of these sins will lead to disastrous and fatal results.

The military is known for its discipline and *esprit de corps*. Everyone respects a disciplined and unified military. We who are believers are also good soldiers. We are under the command of the Lord Jesus Christ. But we also pledge ourselves to follow our Pastor as he follows Christ. How can we stand by our Pastor and serve as good soldiers in the Lord's army?

We Must Be Biblically Faithful

Stand by your Pastor by being steadfast and reliable. Superstardom is not required of everyone but faithfulness is. "You therefore must endure hardship as a good soldier of Jesus Christ. No one engaged in warfare entangles himself with the affairs of this life, that he may please him who enlisted him as a soldier" (2 Timothy 2:3, 4). The good soldier is always true and loyal.

We Must Be Biblical Followers

The first mark of a good soldier is to be a good follower. All good leaders know how to follow a leader. Just as your Pastor follows

Christ and those who are over him in the Lord, so you must pursue this same pattern in your life. The Biblical pattern is to follow your Pastor as he follows Christ. Paul wrote:

♦ "Brethren, join in following my example, and note those who so walk, as you have us for a pattern" (Philippians 3:17).

♦ "And you became followers of us and of the Lord . . . with joy of the Holy Spirit" (1 Thessalonians 1:6).

♦ "For you yourselves know how you ought to follow us, for we were not disorderly among you" (2 Thessalonians 3:7).

We Must Be Biblically Forewarned

Your Pastor is familiar with the strategy of the enemy. Paul warned that Satan will take advantage of us if we are ignorant of his "devices" (2 Corinthians 2:11). Our Pastor reminds us, "We do not wrestle against flesh and blood, but against principalities, against powers, against the rulers of the darkness of this age, against spiritual hosts of wickedness" (Ephesians 6:12). We must put on the whole armor of God described in Ephesians 6, and stand boldly with and by our Pastor.

We Must Be Biblical Fighters

Sometimes the task of a soldier is defending, sometimes it is maintaining order, sometimes it is simply keeping the peace. But a prepared fighter is trained and taught to be aggressive when necessary. He will not cower or retreat in the face of opposition. He will defend his own honor, and the honor of those he is protecting.

Stand by your Pastor by defending him against attacks and criticisms that are untruthful or that belittle his programs and ministry. We must support our Pastor by fighting for truth and right. The Biblical injunction of 1 Timothy 6:12— "Fight the good fight of faith"—is an imperative statement. It is a command, not a suggestion.

I Am a Soldier—With My Pastor

In standing with your Pastor, be determined to be bold, daring, dependable, visionary, trusting and God-honoring. In 1998, Cindye Coates wrote an oft-quoted piece called "I Am a Soldier." I have written this affirmation of loyalty to the pastor, based on that piece:

I am a soldier, a prayer warrior, in the army of my God.
The Lord Jesus Christ is my Commander-in-Chief.
My Pastor is my commanding officer.

The Holy Bible is my code of conduct. Faith, Prayer and the Word
are my weapons of warfare. I have been taught by the Holy Spirit,
trained by experience, tried by adversity, and tested by fire. I am
being led by God and led by my Pastor.

I am a volunteer in this army, and I am enlisted for eternity.
I will either retire in this army at the Rapture or die in this Army;
but I will not get out, sell out or be talked out.
I will be faithful, capable and dependable.

If my God needs me, I am available.
If He needs me in Sunday school to teach children, work with youth,
help adults or just sit and learn; He can use me, because I am there.

I am a soldier, a prayer warrior. I am not a baby.
I do not need to be pampered, petted, primed up, pumped up,
picked up, or pepped up.

I am a soldier, a prayer warrior. No one has to call me, remind me,
write me, visit me, entice me, or lure me.

I am a solider, a prayer warrior. I am not a wimp. I am in place,
saluting my King, obeying His orders, praising His name
and building His Kingdom!
I am following my pastor as he follows Christ.

I am a soldier, a prayer warrior.
No one has to send me flowers, gifts, food, cards, candy, or give me
handouts. I do not need to be cuddled, cradled, cared for, or catered
to. I am committed.

I cannot have my feelings hurt bad enough to turn me around.
I cannot be discouraged enough to turn me aside.
I cannot lose enough to cause me to quit.
When Jesus called me into this army, I had nothing. If I end up
with nothing, I will still come out ahead. I will win.
My God will supply all my needs. I am more than a conqueror. I will
always triumph. I can do all things through Christ.
I am a soldier, a prayer warrior.

People can't disillusion me. Weather cannot weary me. Sickness
cannot stop me. Battles cannot defeat me. Money cannot buy me.
Governments cannot silence me. Evils cannot conquer me and hell
cannot handle me.
I am a soldier, a prayer warrior. Even death cannot destroy me.
For when my Commander-in-Chief calls me from this battlefield, He
will promote me to a captain, and then bring me back to rule this
world with Him.
I am a soldier, a prayer warrior in His army, and I'm marching,
claiming victory. I will not give up. I will not turn around.
I am a soldier, a prayer warrior, marching Heaven bound.
Here I stand! Will you stand with me?

Your Pastor Is a Compassionate Servant-Leader

A faithful servant of God, your pastor also serves the church and
community. In the years immediately following the death and resurrection of Christ, believers were finding their own identity in Christ.
As His followers developed a sense of who they were as Christians,
they were learning from the apostles what it meant to be disciples.

The primary image New Testament believers had of themselves
was a combination of servants of God and servant-leaders for Him.
The idea of servanthood was at the center of their thinking. It colored
everything they did.

> *James, a bondservant of God and of the Lord Jesus
> Christ (James 1:1).*
> *Paul, a bondservant of Jesus Christ, called to be an
> apostle (Romans 1:1).*
> *Simon Peter, a bondservant and apostle of Jesus Christ
> (2 Peter 1:1).*
> *Jude, a bondservant of Jesus Christ, and a brother of
> James (Jude 1:1).*

James felt his primary qualification was his being a servant, not
being the first presiding bishop of the church (see Acts 15:6-13). Paul

boasted of being a servant, not of the churches he organized, the letters he wrote or the missionary journeys he completed. Peter saw his greatest endorsement as being a servant, not his preaching on the Day of Pentecost. Jude could have bragged of his fleshly kinship with Jesus but chose instead to tell people he was Jesus' servant.

Being a servant-leader is not about being a servant *to people*. Rather, it is about being a servant *to God*. Then, because I *am* a servant of Jesus Christ, I am willing to serve anyone in His name. The early believers considered their status as servants to be the most significant aspect of their identity as followers of Christ.

Because we, as members of the church, are undershepherds to our Pastor, we, too, must be servant leaders.

Characteristics of a Servant-Leader

- ◆ He is enthusiastic about the work of God in the church. He meets every challenge with optimism and hope.
- ◆ He is trustworthy in his relationships with people. He is honest and transparent in all his dealings with them.
- ◆ He is self-disciplined in his service to God and to others. One who can conquer himself is qualified to lead others.
- ◆ He is always confident in the way he relates to others. People find it hard to have confidence in one who doesn't have confidence in himself.
- ◆ He is decisive when immediate action is needed. People tend to follow those who are able to make swift and clear decisions.
- ◆ He is courageous when facing the unknown. This does not mean he never has fear; it means he has conquered his fears.
- ◆ He is a friendly and congenial person. He has the ability to see the humorous side of situations and can laugh at himself.
- ◆ He is loyal to the Pastor. He is constant, steadfast, and faithful.
- ◆ He is unselfish in his service to God. Servant-leaders have the ability to forget their own needs in the interest of others'.

Servant and *leader* are equal concepts joined in paradox, not oxymorons. They may be likened to a marriage where two people stand in close proximity to each other, influence each other, and each is incomplete without the other; but in the process neither loses his or her independent identity. This is the Biblical meaning of *servant-leader*.

> *Your attitude should be the same as that of Christ Jesus:*
> *Who, being in very nature God, did not consider equal-*
> *ity with God something to be grasped, but made himself*
> *nothing, taking the very nature of a servant, being made*
> *in human likeness. And being found in appearance as a*
> *man, he humbled himself and became obedient to death—*
> *even death on a cross!* (Philippians 2:5-8, NIV).

Sometimes a congregation can become divided and riddled with tension. In such times, indecisiveness must be transformed into confidence and firmness. The Pastor needs your help and your influence. Many occasions call for tough and quick decisions. We must make a clear distinction between self-interest and community interest. We must be willing to sacrifice our own agendas for the community's good.

A servant is discerning and able to bring out the giftedness in others. He has clearly conquered his own ego needs and prefers that others receive credit which might rightly go to him. He seeks consensus and participation in decision-making. He has the heart of a servant.

To support your Pastor in a servant-leader role, you, too, must be motivated by a sense of calling. In society individualism often replaces community, secular democracy replaces Biblical consensus, and a vote of confidence replaces Biblical accountability. This must not be so in the church. Being a servant doesn't mean turning the church into a shopping mall for consumers of religion. Jesus' disciples are not ushers and waiters in a house of entertainment.

Core Values of Your Pastor

You will know the heart and mind of your Pastor by his core values. These comprise the structure in which he lives and works. Values determine distinctives, direction, development, determination and dedication. The core values of your Pastor tell you what he stands for, what is important to him, what he cares about, and what he will give his life for.

The core values of your Pastor are wrapped around five words: 1) Accountability; 2) Passion; 3) Leadership; 4) Teamwork; and 5) Integrity. Look at some of the virtues these values entail:

1. Total allegiance to God's call on his life.
2. Uncompromising discipline to prayer, sermon preparation, and ministering to the needs of the people.
3. Scripture-based leadership in guiding church members in transforming worship, in utilizing spiritual gifts for significance and service, and in lifestyle evangelism.
4. Coordinated and high-performance teamwork in church ministries based on affirmation, trust and respect for authority.
5. Pure integrity and open transparency in personal conduct, relationships, and commitments.

These core values keep your Pastor going regardless of conditions or circumstances. He is totally given to God's will, and he willingly places himself on God's altar as a "living sacrifice."

Core Values of A Church Member

You can know the depth of dedication of a church member by his core values. Values are the house in which he lives. Values reflect convictions, cooperation, compassion, and commitment. The core values of a church member tell you how seriously he takes the Scriptures, if serving others is a priority, and if spiritual maturity really matters.

Your Pastor has five core values that guide his ministry. For you to find fulfillment in serving God, in working with your Pastor as a partner, and in forming binding relationships with other church members, you must pinpoint core values in your life and live by them. Consider the following ten important values:

1.	Family	6.	Teamwork
2.	Church	7.	Devotion
3.	Commitment	8.	Prayer
4.	Soulwinning	9.	Integrity
5.	Trust	10.	Joy

Now, select five of these values to guide you in building your core values house. After you have selected five values, write out the meaning of each one and how it will be lived out in your Christian life. The following five feeder statements will assist you in developing structure to support your values.

1. **I will exhibit sterling loyalty to God, to my family, and to my church**—"Do not merely listen to the word, and so deceive yourselves. Do what it says" (James 1:22, *NIV*).

2. **I will whole-heartedly worship God "In spirit and in truth" and give myself unreservedly to Him**—"So here's what I want you to do, God helping you: Take your everyday, ordinary life—your sleeping, eating, going-to-work, and walking-around life—and place it before God as an offering" (Romans 12:1, *MSG*).

3. **I will show abundant intensity in stewardship**—"He who sows sparingly will also reap sparingly, and he who sows bountifully will also reap bountifully" (2 Corinthians 9:6).

4. **I will be a source of refreshing to my Pastor**—"A generous man will prosper; he who refreshes others will himself be refreshed" (Proverbs 11:25, *NIV*).

5. **I will maintain intimate fellowship with God through daily prayer, Bible reading, and meditation**—"If you, then, though you are evil, know how to give good gifts to your children, how much more will your Father in heaven give good gifts to those who ask Him!" (Matthew 7:11, *NIV*).

How to Increase Respect for Your Pastor's Calling

♦ **Teach** children about the position and the demanding duties of the Pastor and why they should honor him.

♦ **Show** trust by always being a leader in approving the Pastor's recommendations and programs.

♦ **Focus** attention on spiritual advancements and physical improvements experienced under the leadership of the Pastor.

- ◆ **Display** a spirit of cooperation that is contagious, that cultivates oneness with the Pastor, and that stimulates church growth.

- ◆ **Encourage** church members to show appreciation for the Pastor through special events, gifts, letters, and words of encouragement.

Standing By and With Your Pastor

The calling and character of your Pastor has been outlined. His duties as a shepherd, a soldier, and a servant-leader have been listed. God's plan for you and the Pastor to be partners in ministry has been presented. Now we want to do two things that will connect you with your Pastor's calling: embrace the principles embodied in "I Believe in My Pastor," and adopt the "My Covenant With My Pastor" as a foundational guide in being a co-worker with him.

I Believe in My Pastor

I BELIEVE when I *walk* with my Pastor in Christian mission I can … *Visualize* his God-given plans, help *Actualize* his programs, and *Maximize* my skills in the local church.

I BELIEVE when I *join* my Pastor in worship I can . . . *Anticipate* God's presence, *Cooperate* by being sensitive and receptive, and *Celebrate* God's love and tender care.

I BELIEVE when I *participate* with my Pastor in ministry I can … *Assist* in utilizing all the talents God has placed in the local church, help *Maximize* opportunities to reach and teach, and lead workers to *Realize* their value in the life of the church.

I BELIEVE when I *pray* for my Pastor I can … *Feel* his spirit of ministry, *Ask* God to bless him in specific ways, and *Partner* with him in seeking God's guidance and blessings.

My Covenant With My Pastor

Understanding that it is God's plan for the Pastor and the People to come together as partners, coworkers in the mission and ministries of the local church, I COVENANT:

To **SUPPORT** him with an attitude of congeniality, openness, and cooperation.

To **STRENGTHEN** him with a caring spirit of trust, loyalty, and dependability.

To **STAND** with him in confidence for visionary planning and consistent performance.

To **SAFEGUARD** him with authority against pastoral fatigue and unfounded criticism.

To **SALUTE** him with honor for compassionate leadership and Kingdom achievements.

Signed _____

A Pastor's Prayer of Thanks for Church Members

Thank You for the flock with which You have blessed me. Help me love all the sheep and lambs as You love them, and follow the example that You have set.

Help me sacrifice my own interests, and make the needs of the people my top priority. Let me set the example in giving, for I know that it is in giving that we emulate You.

Let me utilize the abilities You have invested in me to help church members utilize their abilities to grow spiritually, plant the seeds of the gospel, and work in harmony with me in reaping the harvest.

Help me be honest in all relationships, brave in proclaiming Your will and humble in spiritual victories. *Amen.*

A Member's Prayer of Thanks for the Pastor

Thank You for the shepherd with which You have blessed me. Help me love him and his family as You have loved me and as he loves me.

Help me to be willing to sacrifice my way for Your way as You direct my Pastor in the way You have planned for our church. Let me make the giving of myself and of my substance a priority. You have demonstrated that it is in giving that I model Your nature.

Let me utilize my abilities to undergird the Pastor in his plans and to practice personal stewardship in what You have charged me to do. I want to be in harmony with You and my Pastor.

Help me to be faithful in my commitments, consistent in my lifestyle, loyal to my Pastor, and appreciative of the spiritual victories with which You have blessed me. *Amen.*

Invitation to Interaction

1. Discuss why your Pastor's call is the unshakable foundation for his ministry : Appointed, Anointed, Commanded and Commissioned.
2. List, then talk about, five characteristics of a caring shepherd.
3. Read the affirmation, *I Am a Soldier—With My Pastor.* If every person in the congregation embraced this stance, how would it impact your city?
4. Is a servant-leader a servant or a leader? How can he/she be both?
5. How can the core values of your Pastor blend with your core values as partners in ministry?
6. In what ways can the five statements in *My Covenant With My Pastor* bring the church together as a winning team?

CHAPTER TWO

The Pressure of Your Pastor's Ministry

STAND BY YOUR PASTOR

Stand by your Pastor,
Hand in hand to be a friend,
Willing to defend,
And one on whom he can depend.

Stand by your Pastor,
Spreading good news,
Filling the pews,
Compelling the lost to come in.

Stand by your Pastor,
Upholding the truth,
Loving one another,
Doing God's work in the church.

Stand by your Pastor,
Moving the church forward,
Taking a holy stand,
Glorifying God throughout the land.

The ABCs of the Pressure of Your Pastor's Ministry

A – **ANSWERING** questions about spiritual standards.

B – **BELIEVING** God for the needs of the people.

C – **COMFORTING** the sick, homebound, bereaved and dying.

D – **DEALING** with negative attitudes about life and the church.

E – **ENGAGING** the congregation in the Great Commission.

F – **FULFILLING** God's calling to be a shepherd.

G – **GIVING** counsel to youth, the perplexed and the drifting.

H – **HOLDING** the hands of stumbling Christians.

I – **INSTRUCTING** people in Scriptural stewardship.

J – **JOINING** civic leaders to aid in community projects.

K – **KNOWING** how to respond to criticism.

L – **LEADING** believers in total-life commitment.

M – **MOTIVATING** members and involving them in ministry.

N – **NETWORKING** to maintain peace and harmony.

O – **OPERATING** the church office with efficiency.

P – **PROMOTING** expansion and building programs.

Q – **QUESTIONING** leaders about vision and accountability.

R – **REFUTING** critics who seek to divide the flock.

S – **SHOWING** patience in teaching Biblical maturity.

T – **TALKING** to couples about marriage difficulties.

U – **USING** the gifts of all the people in the church.

V – **VIEWING** evangelism outreach from God's perspective.

W – **WRESTLING** with the enemy to bring victory to the church.

X – **EXERCISING** authority to guide in righteous living.

Y – **YEARNING** for renewal and the blessings of God.

Z – **ZEROING** in on fulfilling God's will for the church.

The Pressure of
Your Pastor's Ministry

Statistics compiled by leaders in several different fields conclude that one of the most difficult professions in life is that of a Pastor. A Pastor must represent God to the people and the people to God. He must do this in the context of a holy lifestyle, the heart of a servant, and a mind filled with wisdom that unifies, heals, inspires, and guarantees both spiritual and personal success.

The Pastor must meet the expectations of the people, which vary from family to family, elder to elder, and committee to committee. Every sermon is evaluated and every decision is monitored. He must be up early studying, out in the community visiting, in the hospital comforting, and among the people ministering. He must be all things to all people all the time in all situations. Check the following description of the nature of "A Good Pastor."

A Good Pastor
It has been said that a good Pastor must have . . .
The strength of an ox,
The tenacity of a bulldog,
The daring of a lion,
The wisdom of an owl,
The harmlessness of a dove,
The industry of a beaver,
The gentleness of a sheep,
The versatility of a chameleon,
The vision of an eagle,
The hide of a rhinoceros,
The perspective of a giraffe,
The endurance of a camel,

The bounce of a kangaroo,
The stomach of a horse,
The disposition of an angel,
The loyalty of an apostle,
The faithfulness of a prophet,
The tenderness of a shepherd,
The fervency of an evangelist,
The devotion of a mother.
Even then, he would not please everybody.

The Duties and Demands of a Pastor

When you consider the duties in and demands on the life of a Pastor, are there enough hours in the week to fulfill them? Carefully analyze the following responsibilities and estimate the time it would take to accomplish them. After you have recorded a time in each area, tabulate the total hours required. Often the expectations placed on a Pastor are unreasonable. Some things expected of him are impossible to accomplish.

Awareness Quiz: The Pastor's Responsibilities

These demands are placed on your Pastor's time. Indicate the time you think your Pastor should devote to these activities. Break the hour into smaller segments if you feel it is necessary.

TIME (Hours Per Week)	ACTIVITY\DUTY
_____	Studying for personal, spiritual, and intellectual growth.
_____	Preparing sermons: two for Sunday and a sermon or Bible study during the week.
_____	Preparing worship services, selecting scriptures, hymns, prayer time, order of worship, and so forth.
_____	Preparing new members for baptism and church membership.

_____ Working with Sunday school leaders.

_____ Visiting inactive members.

_____ Visiting the sick in hospitals throughout the city and in their homes.

_____ Visiting the aged and shut-ins.

_____ Evangelistic visitation of prospective new members.

_____ Visiting the bereaved at the time of tragedy or death.

_____ Visiting the bereaved sometime after the death.

_____ Visiting active families of the church.

_____ Counseling church members with practical and emotional problems.

_____ Counseling individuals and families outside the church who ask for help.

_____ Visiting time to soothe "hurt feelings" among members involved in relating to each other.

_____ Attending church committees and board meetings.

_____ Attending church social functions, class parties, ladies' meetings, and so forth.

_____ Meetings with youth, music, lay leaders, and so forth.

_____ Accepting invitations for crusades and speaking engagements in other churches.

_____ Helping in community religious services: Good Friday, Thanksgiving, evangelistic crusades, religious training crusades.

_____ Counseling couples for marriage.

_____ Conducting weddings.

_____ Conducting funerals.

_____ Giving leadership in denominational activities: local, regional, and national.

_____ Speaking at service clubs, commencements, PTA, and other civic organizations.

_____ Serving on boards and committees of church-related institutions—colleges, seminaries and youth camps.

_____ Attending inspirational ministerial conferences and retreats to be revived and minister to others.

——————— Personal and family activities — time with spouse, children, and home requirements.

——————— TOTAL HOURS

A Pastor would have to be super-human to perform all the work outlined. Most Pastors do not have a paid staff to assist them. This builds up additional pressure. And that's not all. He wears chains that place weight and worry on him.

The Chains of Your Pastor

As we continue to look at the pressure of your Pastor's ministry, let us look at the chains your Pastor wears in fulfilling his calling.

The apostle Paul was a Pastor. He planted churches, preached the Good News, and partnered with church members in ministry. His commitment was costly. In fact, it placed him in chains. Look at the following verses:

> *Remember my chains. Grace be with you* (Colossians 4:18).
>
> *I would to God that not only you, but also all who hear me today, might become both almost and altogether such as I am, except for these chains* (Acts 26:29).
>
> *I [wish] to keep [Onesimus] with me, that on your behalf he might minister to me in my chains for the gospel* (Philemon 13).

As we look at the chains of Paul, although in many cases they were literal, they can be used to represent the chains your Pastor accepts in fulfilling his calling as a minister of the Gospel of Jesus Christ.

First, let's look at an acrostic of the word *chains* that sets forth the personal impact of wearing chains for Christ as a Pastor:

C – Confinement
H – Hardship
A – Adjustments
I – Impersonal
N – Numbness
S – Suffering

Look at six restrictions, or areas of confinement to chains, that your Pastor faces:

1. Chains Are IMPERSONAL. *This is a restriction of personal worth.* Paul said, "But whatever things were gain to me, those things I have counted as loss for the sake of Christ. More than that, I count all things to be loss in view of the surpassing value of knowing Christ Jesus my Lord, for whom I have suffered the loss of all things, and count them but rubbish so that I may gain Christ" (Philippians 3:7, 8, *NASB*). This means your Pastor gives up, gives in and gives over his life to share God's grace. His actions are impersonal; he willingly gives himself to ministry without thought of recognition or reward.

2. Chains Mandate CONFINEMENT. *This is a restriction of liberty.* Paul said, "I [am] the prisoner of Christ Jesus" (Ephesians 3:1). In 1 Corinthians 6:12, he said, "All things are lawful for me, but all things are not helpful." Forsaking "all" to perform ministry is an absolute imperative. This means your Pastor cannot go where he wants to go or make his own decisions about duties and directions. He is confined to God's placement.

3. Chains Cause HARDSHIP. *This is a restriction of freedom.* In writing to Pastor Timothy, Paul said, "Suffer hardship with me, as a good soldier of Christ Jesus" (2 Timothy 2:3, *NASB*). The King James Version says, "endure hardness." This means your Pastor must endure the hardships of isolation, complaints, self-appointed crusaders, and the constant schemes of Satan. He must be "watchful in all things, endure afflictions . . . fulfill [his] ministry" (2 Timothy 4:5).

5. Chains Produce NUMBNESS. *This is a restriction of sensitivity.* Paul said, "So that I would not become too proud of the wonderful things that were shown to me, a painful physical problem was given to me. This problem was a messenger from Satan, sent to beat me and keep me from being too proud" (2 Corinthians 12:7, *NCV*). This means that your Pastor has both mental and physical stress from performing ministry. He experiences fatigue, strain, and emotional pressure as he fights the forces of Satan, and as he feeds and leads the forces of faith.

3. Chains Require ADJUSTMENTS. *This is a restriction of security.* "To the weak I became as weak, that I might win the weak. I have become all things to all men, that I might by all means save some. Now this I do for the gospel's sake" (1 Corinthians 9:22, 23). Your Pastor lives a self-emptying, sacrificial and serving life. He makes whatever adjustments are necessary to shepherd and feed the flock he is appointed to watch over.

6. Chains Add SUFFERING *This is a restriction of well-being.* Paul said, "Therefore most gladly I will rather boast in my infirmities, that the power of Christ may rest upon me. Therefore I take pleasure in infirmities, in reproaches, in needs, in persecutions, in distresses, for Christ's sake. For when I am weak, then I am strong," and "I will very gladly spend and be spent for your souls" (2 Corinthians 12:9, 10, 15). This means your Pastor endures hardships of every description to develop you in the ways of Christ — He accepts weaknesses, insults, hard times, and calamities so he can claim God's power to be your caring shepherd.

The apostle Paul was a Pastor; he knew what it meant to wear chains for the sake of the Gospel. Your Pastor accepts chains to fulfill his calling as an appointed minister of the Gospel.

Remember
THE CHAINS OF YOUR PASTOR
— An Opportunity to Serve With Him —

As a church member, you are not asked to wear chains. But, you are called upon to recognize the Pastor's chains and to assist him in not being immobilized by them. Now, we will look at an acrostic of the word *chains* and discuss ways you can stand by your Pastor in ministry, make his load lighter, and reap a greater harvest in the local church for the glory of God:

C – Compassion and Understanding
H – Hold Up His Hands
A – Attitude of Agreement
I – Involvement in Ministry
N – Nurturing Partnership
S – Steadfastness and Accountability

1. COMPASSION and Understanding . Compassion is a tender spirit of identifying with the problems and pressures of another. The source of this tender spirit is understanding. When you understand the demands placed on your Pastor, you stand by him and show empathy, sympathy, gentleness, kindness, and thoughtfulness.

2. HOLD Up His Hands. The story of Aaron and Hur holding up the hands of Moses, their Pastor-leader, is a model for church members today (Exodus 17:10-12). The victory over the Amalekites, the enemy of God's people, was achieved as they held up Moses' hands, one on each side of him. When you faithfully stand by your Pastor, you fortify his faith, strengthen his resolve, refresh his spirit, and celebrate victory with him.

3. ATTITUDE of Agreement. Attitude reflects the content and courage of the soul. Agreement is a key factor in attitude — agreement about church mission, core values, and standards for character and conduct. When you agree with your Pastor, your attitude will be positive, confident, constructive, cooperative, and progressive.

4. INVOLVEMENT in Ministry. Ministry is the business of the church. Involvement is the measuring device that shows how effective the business of the church is. An unwillingness to get involved reduces the flow of faith in the church. When you are involved, the mission of the church is advanced, the ministry of the Pastor is strengthened, and the Kingdom of God is expanded.

5. NURTURING Partnership. The People and the Pastor in the local church are partners in ministry. This is God's plan. The Pastor leads and feeds; the People witness and win. They nurture each other. When you recognize this partnership role in ministry with your Pastor, there is holy harmony, the harvest is reaped together, and the work of God is done with rejoicing, hand in hand with each other.

6. STEADFASTNESS and Accountability. Paul the apostle and Pastor said, "Stand therefore." Then he lists the sixfold elements of Christian armor that will help you to stand (Ephesians 6:14-18). And in 1 Corinthians he admonished, "Watch, stand fast" (16:13). When you stand fast in faith and fruitful service with your Pastor, you accept accountability for church projects. Your service will operate efficiently, smoothly and effectively.

How Do You Rate as a Church Member?

We have considered some of the expectations and chains that place pressure on your Pastor's ministry. It has been pointed out that he is constantly evaluated and monitored. But, what kind of team player are you with the Pastor? Are you a drag or a delight? Are you a giver or a taker? Are you an enabler or a disabler? The following test will reveal your posture with your Pastor.

PERSONAL QUIZ

You can be a major player on the church team with your Pastor. It will require determination, discipline, and the development of support strengths. Read each of the following questions. Check the ones you can answer in the affirmative. Determine your partnership standing, and then work to maintain or cultivate the qualities outlined.

Do I . . .

____ Display a team spirit in working with the Pastor and other church leaders?

____ Show a visionary, upbeat, and enthusiastic attitude about church growth?

____ Seek for win/win situations in church programs and plans?

____ Exercise my spiritual gifts in a Biblical and disciplined manner?

____ Strive to convey a positive spirit of friendliness and concern to other church members and guests?

____ Practice patience in outlining strategies for recruiting and training workers and in planning for the future?

____ Accept accountability when I am given authority in a church project or a leadership assignment?

____ Show excitement in helping set church goals and in working to achieve them?

____ Help other church members discover and utilize their gifts without trying to focus on mine?

____ Show stability in my Christian lifestyle, thereby influencing others to a more constant walk with Christ?

____ Assist in maintaining a healthy, balanced church by sharing goals, concepts, and a sense of shared values?

____ Show care, consideration, compassion, and commitment in my relationship with my Pastor and his family?

____ Project a spirit of receptivity when my Pastor preaches, teaches, and counsels that shows submission and signs of spiritual maturity?

____ Display support for my Pastor through visible and tangible expressions of appreciation?

HOW TO TOTAL YOUR SCORE

Possible score is 98 points. Give yourself seven (7) points for each question receiving an affirmative checkmark. Rate your partnership with your Pastor score:

98 – Par Excellence Partner   77 – Part-time Partner
91 – Pillar Partner   70 – Problem Partner
84 – Productive Partner   63 – Poor Partner

What does your score reveal about you? A poor score could stem from a limited concept of the role of your Pastor and the qualities he should possess.

As we look at the role of the Pastor, we also have to look at the role of the people. This brings the body together to do the work of the church:

PASTOR	*PEOPLE*
P – Proclaimer	**P** – Partners
A – Administrator	**E** – Equippers
S – Shepherd	**O** – Organizers
T – Trainer	**P** – Promoters
O – Outreacher	**L** – Leaders
R – Refresher	**E** – Evangelizers

The Pastor and the People Blessing Each Other

As the Pastor and the people understand the role each one plays, they are in a position to bless each other. This creates a spirit of acceptance and appreciation for different gifts and personalities. The church can then flow in faith and fellowship, and there is happiness and health. When a church is healthy, it will recognize its potential and will flourish and grow.

Blessing Each Other in Love

The Pastor	The People
Blessing the People	Blessing the Pastor
Loving the People	Loving the Pastor
Preaching God's Word	Responding to Sermons
Modeling Scriptural Values	Showing Scriptural Maturity
Guiding in Worship	Attending Church Regularly
Building Family Trust	Building Up Others
Praying for Prosperity	Praying for Togetherness
Leading in Ministry	Participating in Ministry
Pushing for Excellence	Consistently Paying Tithes
Giving Wise Counsel	Supporting Church Programs
Shaping Christian Character	Displaying Personal Trust

You see the spiritual structure of the church when the Pastor and the People are blessing each other, but there is also another scenario. All people who attend church are part of the body. All people, however, do not contribute to the growth and welfare of the body. There are givers and takers, leaders and leaners, and those who are a blessing and those who are a burden. Adopt and practice the characteristics of those who are a blessing and avoid the negatives of those who are a burden.

$\mathcal{A}$ $\mathcal{B}$*lessing or a* $\mathcal{B}$*urden*

Those who are **A BLESSING** see the big picture of the church. They see the many ministries required in fulfilling the Great Commission.

Those who are *A BURDEN* have tunnel vision. They only look in one direction and see a narrow picture of the work of the church.

Those who are **A BLESSING** see the church as a family. They see the importance and value of each member, and they honor the love that binds the family together.

Those who are *A BURDEN* see the church as a supermarket. They pick and choose what appeals to them, and they view the church staff and other members as checkout clerks and individuals to serve them.

Those who are **A BLESSING** see themselves as co-workers, partners, associates with the Pastor. They see the work of the church as "our" mission, "our" ministry, "our" responsibility.

Those who are *A BURDEN* see themselves as employers, supervisors and inspectors of the Pastor. They see the ministry of the church as *his* calling, *his* responsibility, *his* job description.

Those who are **A BLESSING** see involvement in church ministries as a response to divine love and a holy privilege. They give themselves with dignity, integrity and faithfulness.

Those who are *A BURDEN* see the operation of the church from a business perspective, and feel that giving money takes the place of personal participation in ministry.

Those who are **A BLESSING** see the need for the Pastor to have a balanced and nourishing family life. They respect his privacy at home, and facilitate periods of rest and relaxation for him.

Those who are *A BURDEN* see the Pastor's time as their time. They feel his free time should be limited, and he should always be available to meet any need they might have.

Those who are a burden must be led to see the many facets of pressure on a Pastor's ministry. This is one of the purposes of this book. There are many ways to do this and, at the same time, strengthen the support of the Pastor among all church members. Here are some areas to emphasize.

Understand Your Pastor's Ministry

God's call and hand is on your Pastor's life. As you understand the vast scope of his ministry, you are able to enjoy him more, and to be a more effective supporter.

Understanding your Pastor's ministry better and more fully is personally enriching and spiritually strengthening. It will enable you to fulfill your ministry in a better way and enlist more people in supporting the mission of the church.

Resolve to make a conscious effort to understand your Pastor's ministry.

Your PASTOR teaches about great truth:

You can experience new life in Christ!
You can be filled with the Holy Spirit!
You can commune with God in prayer!
You can worship God in spirit and in truth!
You can find fulfillment through church membership!
You can live in God's presence in heaven!

Your PASTOR preaches about great possibilities:

You can walk in fellowship with God and enjoy Him forever!
You can be a gold medal winner in life!
You can develop spiritual gifts and perform valuable service!
You can receive God's abundant unlimited blessings!
You can dream big dreams and achieve worthy goals!
You can be an instrument in the hands of the Master!

Your PASTOR provides guidance in being a great witness:

You can be a loving model to your family!
You can be an influential witness to your friends!
You can show the love of Christ through service!
You can be a champion for the mission of the church!
You can join hands with other believers in outreach evangelism!
You can be a partner with him in ministry!

How to Unlock the Gate of Growth With Your Pastor

It is God's will for the local church to experience consistent growth. There are keys that you can use with your Pastor to ensure balanced, age-level, and healthy growth. As you use these keys, you will be blessed, your Pastor will be blessed, and your church will be blessed.

Believe God with him.	Evangelize the lost with him.
Make decisions with him.	Start projects with him.
Launch dreams with him.	Work ideas with him.
Meet needs with him.	Train workers with him.
Study outreach with him.	Evaluate results with him.
Pray for growth with him.	Explore potentials with him.
Love people with him.	Honor workers with him.
Seize opportunities with him.	Tackle problems with him.
Make contacts with him.	Celebrate gains with him.

How to Be a Ministry-Lifter With Your Pastor

The ministry of the local church is a heavy load! Extremely heavy! Let's consider several factors that make ministry a heavy load:

Ministry is **HEAVY** because it revolves around God's plan to reach the unchurched and give them an "abundant-life" relationship with Him.

Ministry is **HEAVY** because it centers on developing believers to reflect the likeness of Jesus Christ and to become mature disciples.

Ministry is **HEAVY** because it focuses on God's grace to live successfully, with significance, spiritual purpose, and a divine covering.

Yes, the ministry of the local church is a heavy load! Extremely heavy!

The heavy ministry load of the local church begins with your Pastor. He is God-called to shepherd the flock, cast the vision, and provide creative leadership to achieve ministry objectives.

Yes, the ministry of the local church is a heavy load. As stated, it begins with your Pastor. And, many church members leave it there. That's why the average tenure of a Pastor is 2.3 to 3.8 years. That's why nine out of ten churches are ineffective. That's why a majority of churches struggle financially. According to George Barna, that's why there is a shortage of volunteer workers to perform ministry.

What's the answer to this dilemma? How can it be corrected?

God has a plan! It includes every church member. It includes you! His plan is for you to be a Ministry-Lifter with your Pastor; to join your Pastor, to come together with him in ministry.

Here's how you can be a Ministry-Lifter with your Pastor:

LIFT up your Pastor as God's anointed servant to lead the congregation in fulfilling His specific will — plans, purposes, activities — for the local church.

LIFT up the banner of ministry according to the spiritual gift(s) God has invested in you. Be proactive. Be visionary. Be dependable.

LIFT up your voice as a personal witness to the unchurched about God's goodness and grace, in affirmation and appreciation to other workers, and in promotion of the mission and ministries of the church.

Understand Your Pastor Is a Giver

Your Pastor Gives . . .

- ♦ Love for AFFIRMATION.
- ♦ Authority for BELIEF.
- ♦ Truth for CONVICTIONS.
- ♦ Directions for DEDICATION.
- ♦ Reasons for EVANGELISM.
- ♦ Seeds for FAITH.
- ♦ Guidance for GODLINESS.
- ♦ Assurance for HOPE.
- ♦ Encouragement for INVOLVEMENT.
- ♦ Reasons for JOYFULNESS.

- Patterns for KINDNESS.
- Training for LEADERSHIP.
- Appreciation for MOTIVATION.
- Support for NURTURE.
- Knowledge for OPPORTUNITIES.
- Instructions for PRAYER.
- Desire for QUALITY.
- Challenges for RENEWAL.
- Praise for SERVICE.
- Respect for TRUTH.
- Understanding for UNITY.
- Inspiration for VISION.
- Insights for WORSHIP.
- Grace for XENOPHOBIA (and all kinds of fear).
- Example for YIELDING.
- Resources for ZEST.

The Five-Way Test

You can help ease the pressure on your Pastor and give him positive support by remembering the five-way test before filling key leadership positions, involvement in church programs, taking a position, voicing your opinion, or making a decision:

1. Will it build TEAMWORK?
2. Will it nurture UNDERSTANDING?
3. Will it undergird MISSION?
4. Will it enhance DISCIPLESHIP?
5. Will it honor GOD?

Develop a Thankful Attitude

A spirit of thanksgiving bonds individuals together. When a member is thankful for his Pastor, it sets in motion understanding, a willingness to give and take, and a desire to lift up and bless. Be thankful always, for your Pastor. Personalize the following statements. Store them in your heart and keep them fresh in your thinking.

I Am Thankful

I am thankful for my Pastor because he never gives up on me! I struggle and strain, and, as a living sacrifice, I keep falling off the altar. But he keeps on believing in me.

I am thankful for my Pastor because he teaches me that through Christ I can make a difference in this world. I slip and slide, but he keeps holding me up and guiding me forward.

I am thankful for my Pastor because he points me to open doors and instructs me to give my dreams a green light. I stand back and shirk, but he keeps pointing to God's grace and the green light before me.

I am thankful for my Pastor who tells me I can claim God's covenant and live the abundant life. I sometimes slow down or stall, but he keeps fueling my faith and stressing freedom in the Holy Spirit.

I am thankful for my Pastor, and I love him because of his compassion and care; I respect him because of his call and commitment; and I follow him because of his Christlike leadership and courage.

Invitation to Interaction

1. Have the expectations of members regarding their Pastor increased over the years? Why?
2. How can the stance of Part-time Partners, Problem Partners, and Poor Partners be changed?
3. Discuss how Pastor and people can bless each other.
4. What keys unlock the gate of growth with your Pastor?
5. Does the Five-Way Test assist you in giving your Pastor positive support?
6. Comment on the "I Am Thankful for My Pastor" statements.

CHAPTER THREE

Purposeful Partnering With Your Pastor

YOU CAN STAND BY YOUR PASTOR

You can stand by your Pastor,
Holding up his hands,
Serving as a worker in ministry,
According to God's master plan.

You can stand by your Pastor,
Strong in faith and loyalty,
Learning, loving, and leading,
All God's children as royalty.

You can stand by your Pastor,
Interceding on his behalf,
Believing together for leading the flock,
Abounding in faith 'round the clock.

You can stand by your Pastor,
Knowing a spiritual bond will grow,
Letting the Holy Spirit flow,
Giving victory over every foe.

The ABCs of the Purpose of Partnering With Your Pastor

A – **AFFIRMS** spiritual gifts for ministry.

B – **BRINGS** the church body together in mission.

C – **CONTROLS** agendas that blur vision.

D – **DIRECTS** energies for maximum performance.

E – **ENABLES** clear communication in the church.

F – **FULFILLS** the need for personal significance.

G – **GIVES** empowerment to achieve goals.

H – **HOLDS** everyone accountable for effectiveness.

I – **INSPIRES** members to be visionary co-workers.

J – **JAMS** vibrations of conflict and complaint.

K – **KEEPS** everyone on the same ministry track.

L – **LEAVES** the doors of creativity in ministry open.

M – **MOVES** the church to a higher level of devotion.

N – **NULLIFIES** the deceitful traps of Satan.

O – **ORDERS** ministry priorities in a careful way.

P – **PROMOTES** total congregational teamwork.

Q – **QUESTIONS** policies that don't net souls.

R – **RESPECTS** the contributions of everyone.

S – **STOPS** private projects that limit growth.

T – **TIES** cords that bind together in love.

U – **UTILIZES** all the lay power of the church.

V – **VIEWS** the potential for evangelism outreach.

W – **WINS** friends and influence in the community.

X – **EXTRACTS** consistency and faithfulness in service.

Y – **YIELDS** effectiveness in managing ministry goals.

Z – **ZOOMS** and speeds involvement in God's plan.

The Purpose of Partnering With Your Pastor

Partnership with your Pastor is a covenant relationship. God designed this plan for the church to represent Him in achieving His purposes on earth. When this partnership is fully understood both by the Pastor and the people, the church moves forward "like a mighty army." This results in influential harmony and healthy, joyful growth.

In many churches today, however, God's plan is not understood or practiced. These statistics from the Fuller Institute of Church Growth, and the PastorCare Network bear witness to this fact.

♦ *The average tenure of a Pastor in America is 3.8 years. Yet, five years are required to build trust and solid relationships among the people and in the community. Around 55 percent of Pastors transition locations of ministry each year.*

♦ *This year 1,300 Pastors will leave their churches as a result of accusations motivated by self-interest, selfishness and short-sightedness. More than 70 percent of the churches will repeat the process within two years.*

♦ *Pressure, stress and the inability to please members cause 1,200 Pastors to leave the ministry each month due to insufficient pay. Over 65 percent have personal financial problems.*

♦ *The work load of Pastors is staggering: 75 percent spend less than an evening a week with their spouses; 67 percent of spouses are dissatisfied with their marriage.*

♦ *Within five years 67 percent of seminary graduates quit the ministry, and only 50 percent complete their working years as a Pastor. Two-thirds of all church members expect a higher moral standard from their minister and his family than they do from themselves.*

What do these statistics mean? They indicate that a vast number of local churches really never connect with their Pastor. The Pastor and the people do not come together as partners in ministry to do God's work His way, under His guidance.

God's plan must be embraced by both parties. There have been errors and misunderstandings by each one. Some Pastors think they must do everything and some members believe they should. Other Pastors want the church members to do everything while they pray and preach. There must be a balance, and that balance is God's plan of partnership in ministry, coming together as a team to achieve a divine dream.

Moses, the Pastor of the children of Israel, had difficulty comprehending God's partnership plan until he was instructed by his father-in-law, Jethro. Stop and read this account in Exodus 18:13-27. Moses was doing all the planning, teaching, preaching, counseling, visiting, and making all the decisions by himself. Let's review the *conditions* and the *cure*.

The Conditions

Poor Time Management. "The people stood before Moses from morning until evening" (v. 13). The people had to wait on the Pastor to lead and feed them.

Failure to Develop Teachers. "I make known the statutes of God and His laws" (v. 16). Individuals were not trained to teach and share God's Word.

Unwise Use of Energy. "You and these people who are with you will surely wear yourselves out" (v. 18). The skills of the people were not developed and directed to perform service.

Lack of Vision to Delegate. "You are not able to perform it by yourself" (v. 18). There was not an awareness of the power of partnership, delegation and teamwork.

The Cure

Divine Trust. "Stand before God for the people" (v. 19). Depend on God, give the difficulties to Him, trust Him, and seize the opportunities to lead the people.

Develop Leaders. "Teach them the statutes and the laws" (v. 20). Lead a Bible study group and ask God to raise up leaders who know His will and plans and who will stand with you.

Model and Mentor. "Show them the way in which they must walk and the work they must do" (v. 20). Walk the talk. Explain what God wants done and how He wants to accomplish it. Model ministry.

Organize for Action. "Moreover you shall select from all the people … and place such over them to be [leaders]" (v. 21). Divide the people into groups so they can develop relationships and find fulfillment in significant places of ministry. Outline a leadership development program.

When God's plan of partnership is followed, dynamic developments take place: "If you do this thing . . . then you will be able to endure, and all this people will also go to their place in peace" (v. 23). Look at what happens. The Pastor is productive, relaxed and refreshed and the people abide in peace, harmony and fruitfulness.

The draining, complaining situation with Pastor Moses and his people developed from improper views by both. Moses' view was, "It's up to me!" The people's view was, "It's up to us!" God's view was, and still is, "It's up to all of us—Me, the Pastor and the people working together as partners in ministry." Partnership is God's plan for the church.

It is vital to form a correct view of your Pastor. Some common views by church members include:

♦ *Personality View.* He gets along well with people. He's warm and friendly.

♦ *Prestige View.* He's here to please the people, to do what we want done and to maintain a good image in the community.

♦ *Productive View.* He's a hard worker, he gets things done.

♦ *Partnership View.* He's here to fulfill the mission of the church with us as a team. The last view, partnership ministry, is the correct view.

It is also vital that the Pastor form a correct view of working with church members. Some views that exist among Pastors include:

- *Power View.* I'm in control and I will chart the course and make all the decisions.
- *Pleasing View.* I'm here to accommodate the people, to be flexible, and to maintain peace and harmony.
- *Prevailing View.* The church will stand the test and I will weather the storm with the people.
- *Partnership View.* I'm here to experience God with the people and to fulfill His ideal with them as partners in ministry. The partnership view is God's plan for His church.

Like Pastor Moses, the Pastors in the Book of Acts realized they needed partners in ministry. They were trying to do all the work but God had a different plan. Look at Acts 6:2-4, 7.

In these verses we see the apostles, representing Pastors, so burdened down with business and busy work—serving tables—that they were not effective in teaching and preaching. They got together and said, "Hey, let's get the people in the congregation to do the work of the church." They all agreed this was a good plan. The laity became partners with the Pastors. So, they chose individuals who met certain qualifications to serve with them:

- *Good* reputation (relationships)
- *Full* of the Holy Spirit (dedicated)
- *Full* of wisdom (skills to make decisions).

They became partners with the apostles and Pastors, and look what happened:

- *Ministry* — The Word of God spread.
- *Membership* — The number of the disciples multiplied.
- *Magnitude* —Many of the priests were obedient to the faith.

What does this mean? It is a picture of church members:

- We "wait on tables."
- We do the work of the church.
- We are partners with the Pastor.

When we work as partners, we accomplish the same things the church members in Acts achieved. Be happy to "wait on tables," because this is the work of the church. How can we wait on tables as partners with our Pastor, and be effective?

Let's form a picture of a table and use it as an example of how our work is supported, or directed. A table has four legs of support. If we are to be true partners with our Pastor, we must have four "legs" or principles, to support "serving tables" or doing the work of the church.

Leg 1 — Love

Love God—heart, soul, mind, body.

Love the Church—willing to give, like Christ, to the church.

Love the People—touched with the needs and hurts of people.

Leg 2 — Loyalty

Loyalty to the Pastor—partners serving God together.

Loyalty in Stewardship—time, tithe, talents.

Loyalty in Achieving—the mission of the church.

Leg 3 — Learning

Learning Continually—God's Word and will.

Learning About Trends—tactics, strategy, methods.

Learning New Ways—a willingness to embrace change.

Leg 4 — Leading

We Must Be Leaders—in tune with the times.

We Must Be Servant-Leaders—sacrificial and visionary leaders.

We Must Lead with the Pastor—forward, onward, upward.

Christ worked in a carpenter's shop. No doubt He built many tables—strong, sturdy, durable.

Let's be table-builders and table-servers in the church!

We know God has a plan for His church—the Pastor and the people as partners in ministry. We also know we must tap into this plan in order to please Him and to be spiritually productive. How do we do this?

God has set forth laws in His Word that reflect His nature and establish His plans for the church. The truths of His Word transform the way we relate to the church, the Pastor, and to each other, and how we engage in ministry. I want us to consider carefully seven of these laws.

Laws of Partnering
With Your Pastor In Ministry

1. The Law of Loving the Church

Christ loved the church and gave His life to establish it (Ephesians 5:25). The church is the bride and body of Christ. In Him, believers are bound together. God has wrapped His will in the ministry of the church. The church is a redeemed community of saints, a worshiping community, a working community and a witnessing community. A loving, caring spirit in the church expresses the mind and heart of God.

The first law in partnering with your Pastor in ministry is to love the church. A love for the church is reflected in respecting its holy character, responding personally to its mission, and refusing to let things damage the influence of the church. During a pastoral change, a building program, the appointment of leaders, procedural disagreements or personality conflicts, you must not permit any attitude, opinion, discussion or behavior to interfere with your loyalty to the church. Refuse to allow these things to divide the harmony of the church, damage its image or weaken its progress. Love the church as Christ loved it.

2. The Law of Looking Within

The first step to take when looking within is to pray this prayer, "Lord, what do You want to do through me to fulfill the mission of my church?" You must be open to see what God wants you to see—His vision. Then there must be a personal declaration: "I will display a willingness to be a part of the vision. I will practice faithfulness to pursue the vision, and I will project a willingness to partner with my Pastor and other church members to achieve the vision." Your words will determine your work and witness.

Christ said, "You are the salt of the earth" (Matthew 5:13). The church is the salt shaker. Are you stuck in the shaker? Salt must flow inside and outside the church. To be S.A.L.T. requires positive action:

S – Sanctification. Am I pure in my motives and relationships?

A – Affirmation. Do I affirm the work of my Pastor and others?

L – Leadership. Do I develop skills and accept responsibility?

T – Teamwork. Do I stand side by side with my Pastor and other church members to work in harmony, unity and love? This means that your way and the Pastor's way come together to accept God's way. Then you perform God's way as partners.

3. The Law of Letting Go

It has been accurately stated, "Deeds rise to the level of creeds." This brings us back to the first statement in this chapter, "Partnership with your Pastor is a covenant (a creed or belief) relationship." This covenant is with your present Pastor. He is the only one you can partner with in ministry. Like the apostle Paul, you must let go of the things which are behind and reach forward to those things which are ahead (see Philippians 3:13).

Look back, and then leap forward! Don't permit yourself to be locked in the prison of past problems or unfounded philosophies about ministry or Pastors. *Don't let the past poison your potential.* Let go of former bad experiences in the church; let go of hurt feelings created when a Pastor left or when a new Pastor arrived; and let go of unfulfilled expectations based on the Pastor being super-human. Love the church, look within and experience a new flow of energy in your life.

4. The Law of Learning Teamwork

You have read it many times: T.E.A.M.—Together Everyone Achieves More. This is the local church, Pastor and people, together performing God's work in His way. They receive His approval and blessings. Every church should be team-based, with each member filling a position according to his or her skills, passion and talents. Every team has a coach, or leader, to oversee the functions of the team. In the local church this is the duty of your Pastor. He is the team leader and you are a partner with him on the team to achieve God's holy purposes.

"Ten Tips on Teamwork" will provide a solid foundation for building unity in your church:

1) *Share* a common vision and mission.
2) *Stress* personal accountability and stability.
3) *Schedule* consistent training sessions.
4) *Sacrifice* personal goals for team goals.
5) *Sow seeds* of trust and character.
6) *Structure* positive performance procedures.
7) *Search* for new team members.
8) *Safeguard* Biblical principles in relationships and outreach.
9) *Scale* new mountains in ministry.
10) *Speak* words of affirmation and praise.

Team effectiveness is built through understanding, prayer and training. These 10 tips will help build a single team with a single dream. Observe the commitments required to build One Team With One Dream.

One Team - One Dream

We will stand united as God's team,
Filled with daring exuberance,
Achieving a heaven-sent dream.

We pledge allegiance to the team,
Honoring and giving respect,
Always demonstrating our best.

We will combine all our skills,
Championing high ideals.
Spreading contagious zeal.

We will keep the dream fresh and alive,
Bringing others by our side,
Going from good to great,
Covered by God's grace,
Running the heavenly race.

5. The Law of Lifting Up

Lift up your Pastor physically, and lift him up through prayer. Aaron and Hur physically lifted the hands of Moses so he could minister effectively. Read the story in Exodus 17. They stood by him, one on each side (v. 12), until victory was achieved. This is a beautiful description of standing by your Pastor. They knew what the mission was, they communicated with Pastor Moses, they permitted him to sit down and rest, they recognized his limitations (fatigue and weakness), and they lifted up his hands. They recognized God was working through him, but that he needed both spiritual and physical support. They reached out to him in love and obedience. Their pattern is worthy to be embraced. Lift up your Pastor through mission support and acts of kindness and encouragement.

The second way to lift up your Pastor is through prayer. It has been said, "A rising tide lifts all boats." Through prayer, the Pastor is lifted, you are lifted and the church is lifted. The reason for this is that the church comes together in spiritual unity as a team. Look at what happens when you pray for your Pastor.

First, you become a **partner** in his calling; you feel his compassion and see his vision. You receive **blessings** from his anointing; you feel God's approval and covering. There is a sense of belonging. You accept **ownership** in church projects; you feel a sense of accountability and adventure.

Also, you serve as a **role model** for others. You feel joy in helping shape believers into the likeness of Christ. Through prayer you preach, visit, counsel and inspire with your Pastor. In chapter 5, ideas are given for supporting your Pastor through prayer: Pastor's Prayer Team, Prayer Walks, Daily Prayer Guides and Family Prayer.

6. The Law of Leading Others

To be a partner with your Pastor in ministry you must be a follower and a leader. As a follower, you must be consistent in church attendance, advancing in Christian maturity, and demonstrating trustworthiness in using spiritual gifts. The disciples ardently followed Christ; they looked, they listened, they learned. They embraced His concepts and were ready to represent Him when He instructed them to "go, teach, and make disciples." Be a faithful follower—look, listen, learn—and then be a fruitful leader like the disciples of Christ.

What are the marks of a fruitful leader? Paul said, "We have different gifts, according to the grace given us. If a man's gift is leadership, let him govern diligently" (Romans 12:6, 8, *NIV*). Leadership in the church means different things to different people. Basically, it is using God-endowed skills to fulfill the mission of the church. Lead in areas you love. What are you passionate about? What do you enjoy doing?

Leadership is also getting things accomplished through other people. Learn the art of delegation. This enables you to multiply your influence and results. In leadership, develop F.O.C.U.S.: Flexibility, Organization, Confidence, Unity, and Success. Be a faithful follower and a fruitful leader.

7. The Law of Launching Out

You have to step out to find out. Simon Peter discovered this when Christ told him to "launch out into the deep and let down your nets for a catch" (Luke 5:4). Peter hesitated! His response revealed a faulty philosophy: "We (*dependence on personal power*) have toiled all night *(reliance on personal persistence)* and caught nothing (*trust in personal performance*)" (v. 5). But Peter did open his eyes and let down the net. He was introduced to a new, life-changing philosophy—a reliance on God's power and His miracle-working performance.

The ministry of Jesus was a ministry of radical change. He went against traditional patterns, established cultural concepts and cherished worship customs. He said, "I have come that [the people and the church] may have life . . . more abundantly" (John 10:10)— fresher, more creative and challenging. He was saying, "I have come to challenge the church to launch out into the deep, and experience new effectiveness in worshiping Me and in winning the unchurched."

Accept His challenge and do not be afraid of new trends and new methods. Our goal is to please Him and obey His Great Commission. Let us "launch out into the deep" and look at our worship format, the scope of our music, the use of drama, retaining guests, Bible study groups, generational needs, neighborhood outreach, building relationships with the lost, involvement of youth, training children, and developing fully surrendered, devoted stewards. *When we change our minds and methods, we change our church and our effectiveness.*

Change is finding out what God is doing and joining Him. In the Old Testament, God was represented by a cloud and a pillar of fire. When the cloud or pillar of fire moved, the people had to move the Tabernacle (church) to where God was. The church had to adapt to new surroundings, a new environment. God was not at the old location; He was at a new place of potential and opportunities. Move with the cloud, move with God, and be willing to change — to be a part of new things God is doing.

Here are five things you can do with your Pastor to respond to the challenge to "launch out into the deep" in personal ministry:

♦ Program your mind for Spirit-powered ministry.
Never flag in zeal, be aglow with the Spirit (Romans 12:11, *RSV*).
♦ Push yourself to maximize your skills.
A dream comes through much activity (Ecclesiastes 5:3).
♦ Polish yourself to shine with enthusiasm.
I rejoiced with those who said to me, "Let us go to the house of the Lord" (Psalm 122:1, *NIV*).
♦ Perform with excellence, compassion and consistency.
What joys await the sower and the reaper, both together! (John 4:36, *TLB*).
♦ Praise God continually for Biblical success.
Let the Word of Christ dwell in you richly as you teach and admonish one another with all wisdom, and as you sing psalms, hymns and spiritual songs with gratitude in your hearts to God (Colossians 3:16, *NIV*).

Mistakes Church Members Make in Partnering With Their Pastor

The laws of partnering with your Pastor in ministry are Scriptural, sensible and straightforward. They are easy to understand. However, some church members will deny their application, attempt to dilute their meaning and undertake to influence others to go in a different direction. These mistakes are costly to the church. They create division in the congregation, damage to church image and devastation of spiritual morale and wholeness. These mistakes must be recognized and avoided. And they can be!

1. Resistance to affirming the Pastor's call to the local church. "There was a man sent from God . . . to bear witness of the Light" (John 1:6, 7). Some questioned the background and authority of John the Baptist. Some did not like the way he dressed.; others, the way he preached. But he was "sent from God" to do God's work. Regardless of your personal tastes or preferences, affirm God's calling of your Pastor to the local church, whether it is for a season or a lifetime. He is a man sent from God "to bear witness of the Light [Jesus Christ]." Like Jonathan, who "became one in spirit with David" (1 Samuel 18:1, *NIV*), become "one in spirit" with your Pastor.

2. Failure to grasp the meaning of becoming a fully surrendered steward. Look at what God has invested in you — money, management skills and motivational abilities. They belong to Him; He is the owner. Use them to complement His plan for you and your Pastor to partner in accomplishing His work in the local church. You are a co-worker with your Pastor, not a competitor. "Whoever can be trusted with very little can also be trusted with much, and whoever is dishonest with very little will also be dishonest with much. So if you have not been trustworthy in handling worldly wealth, who will trust you with true riches?" (Luke 16:10, 11, *NIV*).

3. Suppress wholehearted participation in transforming worship. You were created to worship God and to enjoy Him forever. Regardless of the failures of church members, leaders, or even Pastors, God calls for, and deserves, your worship. Even if you don't like the tempo or style of the music, or the worship format, God's plan is for you to attend His house to honor Him and participate in wholehearted worship with other believers. "If you enter your place of worship and . . . you suddenly remember a grudge a friend has against you ... leave immediately, go to this friend and make things right. Then and only then, come back and work things out with God" (Matthew 5:23, 24, *MSG*).

4. Inability to blend personal gifts with the Pastor's passion and vision. The church is one body with many members with each member having a vital role to fill. In 1 Corinthians Paul talks about the church and compares the work of members to feet, hands, ears and eyes—each honorable and complementing the others (12:12-21). Members do not select what part of the body they want to be, "But now God has set the members, each one of them, in the body just as He pleased" (v. 18). God also sets the Pastor in the body as His representative to shepherd and feed, and cast the vision for making disciples and expanding His Kingdom. Whatever you may be in the body—feet, hands, ears, or eyes—follow God's plan and blend with the Pastor's passion and vision. This makes a church body connected in obedience and coordinated in love.

5. Misunderstand God's design and resources for the church. God's work is to be done by God's people in direct relationship to God's plan. What is His plan? It is for believers to be fully surrendered stewards and "cheerfully" lay their treasures at the feet of Christ (2 Corinthians 9:7). This requires obedience, sharing, dreaming and courage. We are channels for God's resources, not containers. "Store up for yourselves treasures in heaven. . . . For where your treasure is, there your heart will be also" (Matthew 6:20, 21, *NIV*). We are also told, "Excel in this grace of giving" (2 Corinthians 8:7, *NIV*). God said in Malachi, "Bring the whole tithe into the storehouse [church] . . . and see if I will not throw open the floodgates of heaven and pour out so much blessing that you will not have room enough for it" (3:10, *NIV*).

6. Lack of resolve in modeling and mentoring lay leadership. No doubt you have heard this statement, "I could do anything if I only knew what it was." As a church member you are to do three things: 1) *Minister* with your Pastor as a co-worker; 2) *Model* leadership; and 3) *Mentor* others to become leaders. Leadership has been defined as "influence." You influence through spiritual maturity. The author of Hebrews wrote, "Let us go on to maturity" (Hebrews 6:1, *NIV*). This means we "fix our eyes on Jesus" and "throw off everything that hinders and . . . run with perseverance the race marked out for us" (see 12:1, 2, *NIV*).

7. Unwillingness to be held accountable for involvement in ministry. Christ said, "As the Father has sent Me, I also send you" (John 20:21). Christ was sent to *share* the Good News, to *serve* sacrificially, to *show* forth the love of His Father, and to *shoulder* the weight of the cross. Christ is our leader. We are accountable to follow His example. We, too, must share, serve, show, and shoulder the weight of the cross. Like Daniel, *discipline* yourself to serve with "an excellent spirit" (Daniel 5:12). *Devote* yourself to exceptional service, not just acceptable performance. *Determine* to be accountable to the commands of Christ and "you will abide in [His] love" (John 15:10).

Build a Bridge to Your Pastor

Connecting with your Pastor in mind, motives and ministry results in Kingdom effectiveness. Standing on opposite sides of the river of personal relationship, you cannot see, touch, hear or feel the love and heart desires of each other. In your relationship with your Pastor, you must take the initiative and build a bridge to him! He will respond. He will meet you more than half way; you can count on it. His arms are outstretched to embrace you. In building a bridge to, or with your Pastor, three points must be considered:

1. **A Bridge Must Be STRONG.** Remember, a bridge is designed to drive on and walk on. The structure must be steady. It must be able to withstand pressure, storms, sleet, snow, rain and hail. Look at the Brooklyn Bridge and the Golden Gate Bridge. A bridge to your Pastor must be STRONG. It must stand the test of time, leadership changes, unfavorable circumstances and internal conflict.

2. **A Bridge Must Be SAFE.** There cannot be daily questions about safety and security—the condition of the support system, wear and tear, or the number of people driving or walking on the bridge. A bridge to your Pastor must be SAFE, providing a sense of security—trustworthy, dependable and honorable.

3. **A Bridge Must SERVE.** A bridge must always be accessible, open. It must connect to something and lead to somewhere. It must serve all types of vehicles and people without restrictions. A bridge to your Pastor must SERVE, bringing people and services together — joyful fellowship, Kingdom service, and God-honoring stewardship. Build a bridge to your Pastor that is strong and safe, and one that serves.

A Picture of Your Pastor

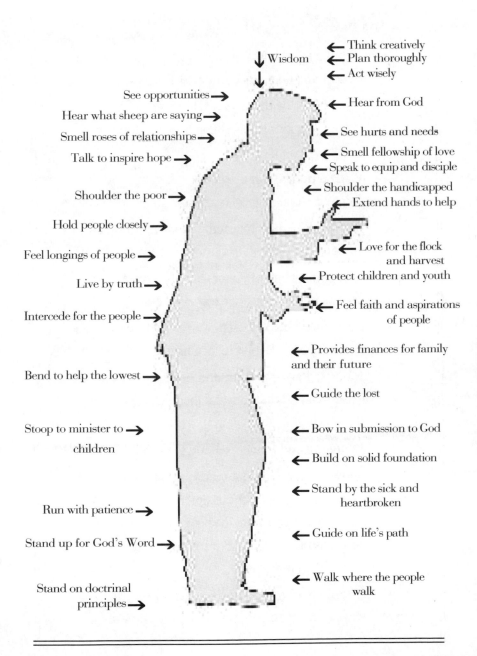

How to Bring Out the Best in Your Pastor as a Partner in Ministry

- Believe that he is committed to bringing out the best in you and expect the best from him.

- Specialize in the areas where your Pastor is strong—maximize his strengths and minimize his weaknesses.

- Place a priority on open, honest, clear, and consistent communication with him.

- Participate wholeheartedly in worship services and give rapt attention during his sermons.

- Compliment him often for church outreach, visionary leadership, and civic achievements.

- Recognize that the most powerful influence on your Pastor is your soul on fire for Christ and His church.

- Join the Pastor's team and believe that church leaders can produce beyond their normal capacity.

- Reveal to him your capacity for remarkable stretching and power waiting to be released.

- Show your Pastor that you want him to succeed. Embrace his goals with contagious enthusiasm. You can get what you want in church life if you help your Pastor get what he wants under the leadership of the Holy Spirit.

- Establish an image of dependability. Let your Pastor know he can always count on you.

A Picture of Church Members

Insight

← Understanding
← Undergirding
← Unity

See mission of church →
Hear voice of →
unchurched
Smell flowers →
of belonging
Talk to →
encourage
Shoulder →
responsibility
Hold →
people closely
Embrace →
other members
Feel the passion →
of the Pastor
Gird with God's →
Word
Equipped to →
reap the harvest
Bond in daily →
prayer for the Pastor
Run with →
determination
Stand up for children →
and youth
Walk where the Pastor →
walks

← See potential of church
← Hear Pastor's message
← Smell beauty of harmony
← Speak to affirm
← Shoulder hurts
and needs
← Love with a
spirit of
sacrifice
← Feel the
power to
perform

← Fully surrendered
steward
← Lead with
compassion
← Bow in intercessory
prayer
← Feet planted on solid
doctrinal foundation

How the Pastor Brings Out the Best in You as a Partner in Ministry

1. HE affirms your value as a member of the family of God and as a significant member of the local church.
2. HE leads you in exalting the Lord in worship and experiencing His presence and the demonstrations of His power in daily life.
3. HE intercedes for your spiritual and physical health, spiritual contentment, and abiding peace.
4. HE guides you in discovering, developing, and deploying your spiritual gifts.
5. HE opens the truths of the Bible so you can understand and reap the fullness of God.
6. HE directs you in avenues of ministry so you can accomplish the mandates of Christ to share the good news, feed the hungry, care for the poor, and lift up the weak.
7. HE expresses pastoral love to you through encouragement, care for your family, and validating your personal worth.
8. HE serves as your shepherd to oversee your security in Christ and guide you on the path of spiritual and financial prosperity.

The Power of a Pledge to Be a Partner With Your Pastor

A pledge is both a *bridge* and a *bond*. It serves as a *bridge* to bring people together and to clarify and cement objectives and standards.

A pledge also serves as a *bond* that unifies faith, feelings, and the functions of the church.

Let's look at ways a pledge between the Pastor and the People, and the People and the Pastor, can facilitate God's work in the local church.

— Ministry Pledge —

A Pledge by the Pastor to the People – I PLEDGE:

To recognize the People of the church as God-gifted and Spirit-empowered to join me in exalting Christ and expanding His Kingdom through the ministries of the local church.

To maintain closeness with my Heavenly Father through prayer, personal holiness, and study in order to feed and lead the People in paths of righteousness.

To cast a vision of the abundant life in Christ, and the mission of the church, that will bless the People and stretch their faith to boldly claim God's promises and power.

To manifest a cooperative spirit, a compassionate attitude, and an expanding commitment to all the age groups of the church so as to undergird their development in Christlikeness.

A Pledge to the Pastor by the People – WE PLEDGE:

To join with our Pastor as partners and co-workers in fulfilling the mission of the local church.

To embrace the Pastor's vision for discipleship and stewardship with Scriptural understanding and congregational unity.

To engage in prayer every day for the ministerial effectiveness, spiritual balance, and physical health of our Pastor.

To accept ministry assignments and to be responsible for consistent service and disciplined conduct.

Think With the Pastor

Learn to THINK with the Pastor. This provides *insight* for you and *inspiration* for him. The Pastor is THINKING about:

Sermons: What is God leading me to share with the people?

Relationships: How can I better understand and bond with others?

Prayer: How can I present the needs of the people to God?

Worship: By what means can I intensify true worship?

Ministry: What programs can I sponsor to equip disciples?

Outreach: How can I be more effective in reaching the community for Christ?

Stewardship: How can I lead the people to be faithful in tithing?

Evangelism: What plans can I implement to stress personal soul winning?

Unity: What can I do to maintain and strengthen the unity of the church?

Family: How can I mold and protect the families of the church?

Activities: What events can we sponsor to activate Christian service?

Study: How can I guide the people in a program of consistent Bible study?

Praise: How can I direct the people in being positive and thankful!

An Invitation to Interaction

1. Look at the Conditions and the Cure of the situation faced by Pastor Moses. Talk about what took place.

2. How was the problem of leadership in the Book of Acts solved?

3. Discuss the Law of Letting Go. How can holding on to the past poison a church member's potential?

4. Why is it important to affirm your Pastor's call to the local church?

5. In partnership, each person should bring out the best in his partner. What are the advantages of this?

6. In what ways is a pledge both a bridge and a bond?

CHAPTER FOUR

The Process of Standing By Your Pastor

WE WILL STAND BY OUR PASTOR

We will stand by our Pastor,
Understanding we both are called,
Sharing His life-giving laws,
Seeking His promises and power to fall.

We will stand by our Pastor,
Passionately winning the lost,
Discipling and baptizing,
Never once counting the cost.

We will stand by our Pastor,
With God's tools in our hands,
Like Nehemiah's hard-working band,
Building for eternity our land.

We will stand by our Pastor,
Touching the staff in his hand,
Walking together with our Shepherd,
Enjoying the fruit of God's plan.

The ABCs of the Process of Standing by Your Pastor

$\mathcal{A}$ – **ACCEPT** his personality and style of leadership.

$\mathcal{B}$ – **BELIEVE** God wants to speak to you through your Pastor.

C – **COMMIT** questions and reservations to God in prayer.

$\mathcal{D}$ – **DEVELOP** trust, confidence, and loyalty to him.

$\mathcal{E}$ – **EXAMINE** your skills and spiritual shortcomings.

$\mathcal{F}$ – **FOCUS** on your responsibilities as a church member.

G – **GROW** in fellowship through care and kindness.

$\mathcal{H}$ – **HOLD** up your Pastor as a man sent from God.

I – **INCLUDE** your family in discussing his workload.

J – **JUDGE** yourself on the same basis as you judge your Pastor.

$\mathcal{K}$ – **KEEP** the mission of the church in clear focus.

$\mathcal{L}$ – **LOOK** at the positive qualities of his ministry.

M – **MOVE** to a higher level of serving as a co-worker.

$\mathcal{N}$ – **NOTARIZE** God's call to come together and minister.

O – **ORGANIZE** your vision to flow with your Pastor's vision.

$\mathcal{P}$ – **PROMOTE** events that bond and breed understanding.

Q – **QUICKLY** seize opportunities to encourage and assist him.

$\mathcal{R}$ – **REFUEL** your faith often for maximum performance.

S – **SUBMIT** to Biblical authority cheerfully.

$\mathcal{T}$ – **TEST** your own effectiveness as a leader.

$\mathcal{U}$ – **UNTIE** cords that interrupt teamwork.

V – **VERSE** by verse let the Bible speak about partnership.

W – **WIN** in the community by having a winning church team.

$\mathcal{X}$ – **EXPRESS** appreciation and honor openly and often.

$\mathcal{Y}$ – **YEARN** for renewal in the church with your Pastor.

$\mathcal{Z}$ – **ZIP** up the garments of praise for God and each other.

The Process of
Standing by Your Pastor

Standing by your Pastor is a major spiritual decision! It is made in consideration of God's will for the local church, personal obedience to His plan and commitment to fulfill the Great Commission.

Standing by your Pastor is also a process. It includes understanding each other's personalities, agreeing on the best discipleship programs for the church and coming together as partners in ministry.

In this chapter we will feature profiles of church members and Pastors. This is not to show division in the church, but to emphasize that we all are different, that we have to recognize and honor those differences, and that we must come together in both belief and unity to be effective witnesses for Jesus Christ. Biblical methods and action steps to achieve these objectives are also set forth.

Pastors, like church members, come in varied styles and interesting personalities. Both the admirable clergy and the wonderful laity come from all walks of life and display varied gifts and personalities. They come from different backgrounds. The awesome miracle is that God can take this diverse group and make it into an effective and dynamic team to do His work. In the New Testament Peter, a fisherman; Matthew, a tax collector; Luke, a physician; and Paul, a tent maker all became a part of the coalition of faithful believers. So today ministers and members who come from all occupations and walks of life, make up the ranks of God's victorious church.

Mutual respect for each other and our roles is an imperative if we are to come together as God's people. When we live out the principles of the Kingdom, they motivate us to maximize each other's strengths and minimize each other's weaknesses. To be effective in ministry, we have to grow as individuals and adjust to each other's gifts as the Holy Spirit has endowed us individually. We must learn to blend our respective strengths. Both Pastor and parishioner follow the same path. They may take different steps to get there, but both are working toward the same goal—the growth of God's Kingdom.

When members and Pastors misunderstand each other's roles and personalities, mistrust results. The church is never as effective as God wants it to be. Failing to understand one another leads, inevitably, to conflict and disharmony. My heartfelt desire is to facilitate an ongoing dialogue between pulpit and pew so that we can all understand better our tasks in the great work of building the Kingdom.

Profiles of Different Church Members

In 1 Corinthians 12, Paul outlines unity and diversity in the body of Christ, the church. He says, "God has set the members, each one of them, in the body just as He pleased" (v. 18). As we discuss the characteristics of different church members, remember God is "pleased" with them all and has set them in the church to accomplish His purposes. Remember, too, "that there should be no schism in the body, but that the members should have the same care for one another" (v. 25).

1. THE MOTIVATED MEMBER

The Motivated Member looks at every situation, no matter how smooth or difficult, and announces, "Give me this mountain!" Daring, bold, full of faith and self-confident, he has a cause and a goal. He is truly among the giants of the church.

Remember Caleb? The conquest of Canaan was complete. General Joshua had led God's people across the Jordan River, past Jericho and Ai. They had defeated every enemy before them. Their motto could have been the immortal words of Todd Beamer, "Let's roll!"

By now, however, the victorious people were weary. They were ready to rest. But not Caleb! He had a goal toward which he had been moving for 45 years. Hear his words to Joshua:

> Moses swore on that day, saying, "Surely the land where your foot has trodden shall be your inheritance and your children's forever, because you have wholly followed the Lord my God." And now, behold, the Lord has kept me alive, as He said, these forty-five years . . . and now, here I am this day, eighty-five years old. As yet I am as strong

this day as on the day that Moses sent me . . . Now therefore, give me this mountain of which the Lord spoke in that day (Joshua 14:9-12).

Some Strengths of the Motivated Member. Like Caleb, Motivated Church Members follow the Lord wholeheartedly. They never give up on the promises of God, never lose their vision and enthusiasm, and are always ready for a new challenge. They accept assignments and follow through completely. They are self-starters, always ready for action. You often hear them say, "Give me another challenge!"

For its survival the church must have these members. They set an example for others to follow. They are the backbone of the church.

Some Weaknesses of the Motivated Member. Sometimes they are lacking in the ability to equip others. Because they are so accustomed to doing things themselves, they may not see the need of equipping other believers. They often have no time for personal devotions. They sometimes tend to get ahead of the Pastor and the church.

2. THE MESSAGE MEMBER

The watchword for the Message Member is, "Preach the Word!" He encourages his fellow members, "Let's turn the speaker loose. He preaches the Word; the Word has the answer!" This Member wants more sermons, deeper sermons and longer sermons. His primary concern is to protect the truth. The Message Member knows the Word and never tires of hearing it preached or taught. Pointing out that Jesus preached (Romans 16:25), he often quotes 1 Corinthians 1:21: "Since . . . the world . . . did not know God, it pleased God through the foolishness of the message preached to save those who believe."

Apollos was a man who loved the message. Eloquent in speech and "mighty in the Scriptures," he knew the ways of the Lord very well (Acts 18:24). He was enthusiastic and taught the Word with care and precision (v. 25). Bold and teachable (v. 26), he volunteered his services to the disciples and was a great help to the early church (v. 27).

Some Strengths of the Message Member. The church desperately needs this type of member. They protect the Word and develop others in the faith. They help the Lord's disciples fulfill the

Scriptures. Their constant concern is for more Bible teaching and study courses. They want the entire body of believers to accept the truth of the Word, and they want God's men to preach every truth in it. Their great desire is for the people of God to know what they believe.

Some Weaknesses of the Message Member. Message Members often look for answers without putting forth any personal effort. They sometimes fail to apply the Word to real life. They believe in feeding, feeling, leading; they want to get bigger without sharing, caring, and reaching. Sometimes they neglect to dress their zeal for the Word in shoe leather. Message Members can be deficient in these areas.

3. THE PRECIOUS MEMORIES MEMBER

The watchword of the Precious Memories Member is, "I remember when. . . ." He describes in vivid detail how it was when people "really" served the Lord. He remembers fondly when the church was full and running over. His perception of the past is that there were miracles every day. He often pays tribute to the faithful members who blazed the trail. He recounts the time when the power of God fell at every service, and signs and wonders occurred on a regular basis.

Some Strengths of the Precious Memories Member. The Precious Memories Member helps us to remember our heritage and the pioneers who blazed the trail before us. He prompts us to honor the leaders of the past. This important member reminds us that history always paves the way to the future. To get the proper perspective on where we are going, we must recall where we have been. He keeps before us the truth that those who have died in the faith are the foundation for what we are today.

Some Weaknesses of the Precious Memories Member. These members sometimes paint unrealistic and flawed pictures of the past. They forget that things were not always exactly as our selective memories recall them. They live in yesterday's environment, ignoring the changing world and circumstances around them. They try to recreate yesterday's glory in today's reality.

Remembering their own leadership in yesterday's revivals, they parrot the phrase, "Do what you've always done, and you'll get the

same kind of response." Some of the greatest hinderers to revival today are the leaders of the revivals of yesterday. They find it difficult to "forget those things which are behind" and move on with God.

4. THE MAINTENANCE MEMBER

The watchword of the Maintenance Member is, "We need quality, not quantity." His cry is for the church to focus more on our own people. "Sure, people are hurting in other places, but look at what we need to do for our own families," he often emphasizes. "We've got a good, solid church. We've got a good structure; we just need to work it. We're strong and solid today; we'll be strong and solid tomorrow!"

Some Strengths of the Maintenance Member. Maintenance Members bring a necessary and needed emphasis on caring for our children, our youth and our adults. To his credit, he emphasizes building on a solid, steady foundation. Prominent among his many strengths are the qualities of durability and faithfulness.

Some Weaknesses of the Maintenance Member. Too often he fails to see the harvest waiting to be reaped. He is usually content with the status quo ("We've always done it this way"). He doesn't like change, and often resists it. Maintenance Members have a definite need for renewed vitality and a new vision that will enlarge their horizons.

5. THE MISSIONARY MEMBER

The watchword for the Missionary Member is, "Win the lost at any cost." This is the person who believes strongly in the Great Commission and makes every effort to fulfill it. Home missions, global missions, evangelism breakthrough — let's do it all. Let's go after the lost. Let's go into the jails, prisons, nursing homes — everywhere! We are commissioned and we are empowered, so there is no reason we can't do everything!

Missionary Members are like magnets; they draw people to them through evangelism. Motivated by the Great Commission, they buttonhole people and tie them down with Scriptures.

Some Strengths of the Missionary Member. Missionary Members keep the Great Commission before the church. They remind us that it is the responsibility of every believer to witness by our words and actions. They keep the focus of the church clearly in view. These people are really the future of the church.

Some Weaknesses of the Missionary Member. Their over-zealousness can turn people off. Too often they forget about teaching, training and discipling new believers. They are often weak on follow-up and in developing disciples. Their vision of the church can be one-dimensional: they often fail to see the big picture.

6. THE MOBILE MEMBER

The watchword for Mobile Members is: "I want my needs to be met." They have what is called the "Multiple-Member Syndrome" (MMS). They feel comfortable in, and are known in, two or three different churches. "Oh, I like my church; I belong here," they often say, "but I have a wide range of interests." If the church down the street is having an event or meeting they like, that is where they will be. If the big meeting or event is occurring in your church, and they perceive their needs will be met there, they will be with you. Their self-justification: "Other people at other churches help me; they understand me. . . ."

Some Strengths of the Mobile Member. Mobile Members prompt the church to foster an ongoing evaluation of its activities and programs. They inspire better follow-up in the church's to-do list. They motivate the congregation to ask: Are we providing for the total needs of our members and our community? Can we do better than we are doing?

Some Weaknesses of the Mobile Member. Mobile Members are often guilty of failing to face reality. They don't accept personal responsibility for anything connected with the church. Consequently, they don't establish much trust as members. By neglecting faithfulness and commitment to a cause, they set an unscriptural example.

7. THE MUSIC MEMBER

The Music Member is the one whose solution for any need or problem in the church is found in music. *If we do the music right, everything else will fall in place*, they reason. Forget everything else, concentrate on the music! Citing the unique example of Jehoshaphat (see 2 Chronicles 20), the Music Member has adopted the watchword, "Let's sing our way to victory."

Some Strengths of the Music Member. Music is one of the most important ingredients in personal and corporate worship. The Music Member helps keep a happy, singing, victorious worship style in the church. These members remind us of our responsibility for regular "psalms and hymns and spiritual songs, singing and making melody in your heart to the Lord" (Ephesians 5:19).

The responsibility of the church to develop music programs that are available to all age groups and cross-section of the church is vital. No church can experience balanced growth without a well-developed music program. The Music Member is important in this endeavor.

Some Weaknesses of the Music Member. Focusing primarily on music pigeonholes a church member and places him in a box. He can become single-dimensional because other aspects of God's gifts to him are not properly developed. While it is true that music can "soothe the savage beast," it is also true that music, with siren voice, can lure pilgrims to their destruction on the shoals of single-issue thinking.

Focusing only on music, or any other single issue, can curb creative thinking in other areas of church life.

Coming Together as God's Team

It is God's will for all church members, though different in spirit and style, to come together as a team. It is important for everyone to combine their skills for the advancement of His kingdom. The premise for doing this is to stand on the same foundation — to have a firm and stationary base of belief and belonging. Each church member should personally adopt the Church Member's Pastoral Creed.

"You are Christ's body—that's who you are! You must never forget this"
(1 Corinthians 12:27, *MSG*).

Church Member's
Pastoral Creed

I BELIEVE the Pastor is called of God, anointed by the Holy Spirit, and commissioned to bear witness of the life, death and resurrection of Jesus Christ, our Lord and Savior.

I BELIEVE the Church was established by Jesus Christ for the coming together of His people to worship Him and to fulfill the Great Commission, and that the Pastor is the spiritual leader who oversees this ministry in the local congregation.

I BELIEVE that church membership identifies an individual as a committed follower of Christ, and that it provides the spiritual structure to develop and demonstrate the true characteristics of discipleship in daily life.

I BELIEVE it is my responsibility to fully embrace the spiritual authority of the Pastor, to support him with respect and consistent stewardship, and to pray regularly for him, his family, and the effectiveness of his ministry.

Bringing Out the Best in
Other Church Members

As you recognize the qualities and contributions of other church members, you should strive to be a true team player. Victories are to be enjoyed by all the members. One way to do this is to purpose to bring out the best in your fellow believers. Here are some ways to do this:

1. Anticipate that other church members will bring out the best in you. Therefore, always expect the best from them.
2. Focus on the areas where they are strong. Maximize their strengths and minimize their weaknesses.
3. Place a high priority on open, honest, consistent, and clear communication.
4. Participate wholeheartedly in worship services. Demonstrate sterling convictions and convincing commitment.
5. Compliment leaders and workers often for their visionary and sacrificial service.
6. Help create an environment where failures become stepping stones for future success.
7. Believe that, through trust and confidence, other team players can be productive beyond their normal capacity.
8. Help create an atmosphere of openness, expectation, and excitement. Rejoice together with other team members, and cherish peak experiences.
9. Establish an image of loyal dependability. Let other church members know they can count on you.

Profiles of Different Pastors

The apostle Paul said, "You are the body of Christ, and members individually" (1 Corinthians 12:27). When we considered the profiles of different church members, we saw unity and diversity in the body. As "God has set the members, each one of them, in the body just as He pleased" (v. 18), so those Pastors whom He places in the church are set there as He pleases.

All Pastors are called and anointed by God, regardless of their personal mannerisms or operational methods. "And [God] Himself [called] some to be apostles, some prophets, some evangelists, and some pastors and teachers" (Ephesians 4:11). Why did God call Pastors?

For the equipping (perfecting) of the saints (church members) for the work of ministry (service), for the edifying (building up) of the body of Christ, till we all come to the unity of the faith and of the knowledge of the Son of God, to a perfect (mature) man, to the measure of the stature of the fullness of Christ" (vv. 12, 13).

Pastors are different from each other in spirit and style, but their responsibilities under God are the same. The Pastor's mission is to guide church members in peace and unity, and help them grow into the fullness of Christ. When this concept is understood, we embrace our Pastor as a unique part of the church. Look at these Pastor profiles.

1. THE PROFESSOR PASTOR

The Professor Pastor has studied God's Word and teaches it well. He believes in explaining both Hebrew and Greek in his well-prepared messages. He believes people become mature in Christ by studying. He preaches expository sermons and they are rich. He often begins with, "Open your Bibles. . . ."

This Pastor puts strong emphasis on Wednesday night Bible study—which he usually leads. He has a passion for unadulterated truth. He often says Sunday school prepares one for a new life founded on God's Word. He emphasizes constantly the importance of knowing what God says in His Word. Professor Pastor staunchly defends the faith.

Ministering With the Professor Pastor. Here are three ways you can effectively support the ministry of the Professor Pastor:

- Check your Bible reading and study habits. Are you consistent in applying God's Word?
- Join a Sunday School class or Bible study group. Build relationships with others who love the Word.
- Pray for Scriptural insight. Memorize Scriptures. Pray, "Lord, lead me by Your Word."

2. THE PLATFORM PASTOR

The Platform Pastor is always at center stage. He is in the spotlight, leading worship, and, by extension, leading the church. He makes all of the announcements, and is faithful to keep the congregation abreast of the parish news. This pastor always prays for the sick and always prays the pastoral prayer. The spotlight is always on him.

The Platform Pastor is important because he is the identity for the Sunday program. He is not reticent or reluctant, but boldly takes charge and comes with a word from God. "The Lord told me to tell you" is a phrase heard often on his lips. Without a tinge of doubt in his speech, he declares that your needs will be met today: "I believe God is going to do this," "God spoke to me about this service."

This personable Pastor preaches strongly. His sermons are often long but they are always tops. The focus is always on him; he is a platform performer.

Ministering With the Platform Pastor.

◆ Have an open, receptive spirit towards him and the work of the Lord. Pray "Lord, fill me with an accepting, receiving spirit."

◆ Avoid criticism. Recognize that his motives and methods are real and authentic; in this way God has gifted him.

◆ Help him build programs that will take a person from the sanctuary into servanthood through training, involvement, and relationships.

3. THE PROGRAM PASTOR

The Program Pastor is a purpose-driven Pastor. He firmly believes that the church must have all kinds of programs to reach all kinds of people. For this reason, he concentrates on putting all of the gifts in the church to work through activities, events and specialties. He designs programs and ministries to reach the outcast, the downcast, the upcast and the "plaster-cast." He promotes with every available avenue and method—cups, banners, pennants, pens and anything else to let people know who the church is and what it is doing.

Ministering With the Program Pastor.

◆ Appreciate the vision of the Program Pastor. Look at the results of his ministry.

◆ Test your own gifts, and make sure you are involved in the ministry of the church. You may discover that God is opening up a new area of ministry for you.

◆ Help to advertise the programs and ministries of the church. Get all excited; go, tell everybody.

4. THE PROSPERITY PASTOR

The watchword for the Prosperity Pastor is, "God wants you to be healthy, wealthy and wise." He emphasizes putting faith to work on a regular and consistent basis. Since God said, "Test Me," let's do that by believing God and stepping out in faith. We can build. We can have a radio/TV program. Our families can be happy. We can build the faith of our people. Let's attempt great things for God. The Prosperity Pastor preaches on victory, overcoming, receiving, planting seed faith, and reaping financial and physical harvest.

Ministering With the Prosperity Pastor.
♦ Understand that God wants to bless all of His children.
♦ Encourage planning for discipleship training and community service.
♦ Express thanksgiving for your abundant blessings. Share testimonies of God's goodness to others whose faith may not be developed quite as much.

5. THE PARTNERSHIP PASTOR

The Partnership Pastor believes God has called the church and Pastor to work together. Like Moses, he understands that he cannot do the work alone, and needs Aaron and Hur (Exodus 17:8-13). Remember Rephidim? Atop a hill overlooking the battle field, Moses stood with Aaron and Hur, raising "the rod of God"(v. 9). When he held his hands high, the battle went for the people of God; when he lowered his hands and the rod, the enemy prevailed. Finally Moses tired and was unable to hold his hands up. So Aaron and Hur sat him down and held his hands up until the victory could be won.

The Partnership Pastor empowers members of the congregation to serve. He depends on their assistance in ministry. He gives them responsibilities for leading and for gaining victories. He shares his ministry and his glory. He honors his partners in ministry as they plan together and pray together. The Pastor and church that partners together in ministry stays in harmony and causes the church to grow in love.

Ministering With the Partnership Pastor.
♦ When asked, accept responsibility in a particular ministry.

- Help build a spirit of teamwork. Here's a helpful acronym—
  T.E.A.M. Together Everyone Achieves More.
- Honor workers on the team. Celebrate team victories together.

6. THE PATRIARCH PASTOR

The Patriarch Pastor is a father-figure to the congregation. He touches everything and everyone. He is always available to drive the bus, cook the chicken or run the bulletins. He speaks to everyone in town; he is known at the funeral homes and in all the community gathering places. He loves to recognize the church's patriarch families, and gives them much authority.

Ministering With the Patriarch Pastor.

- Appreciate him for his hard work. He builds relationships, an important ministry in the Kingdom of God.
- When asked, work on committees. Help spread the workload around. Assist in creating vision in the church.
- Recognize the value of community outreach. Nurture your relationships with community leaders.

7. THE POSITION PASTOR

The Position Pastor knows he is called by God to pastor. "This is a holy position," he often says publicly, and he believes he is here to help you find God's will. He has a "this-is-how-to-do-it" style. He shows you the way. This Pastor builds a foundation for two-to-four years, and then his work is done. He feels other people need him. He is good at short-range goals. He has had a lot of different experiences, and he has faced a lot of different problems.

Ministering With the Position Pastor.

- Understand that your church might need short-range goals at this time. Taking smaller steps under different Pastors may lead to larger steps with other Pastors.
- Help set goals beyond a two- or four-year pastoral tenure.
- Help organize youth programs. Prepare the youth for the future. Sit tight. Be faithful.

When we studied the profiles of different church members, it was both strongly and Scripturally emphasized that we must come together with each other and with the Pastor. Teams combine different skills for the advancement of the Kingdom of God. The foundation for doing this was the Church Member's Pastoral Creed (p. 90).

On the other hand, each Pastor must recognize the different gifts of church members and bring the people together as a worshiping, serving community. The foundation, or base, for him to do this is found in The Pastor's Creed. When both Pastor and member commit to each other, this produces a dynamic unity in the local body of Christ. This kind of synergy makes it possible to challenge the very gates of hell.

The Pastor's Creed

I am committed to being

God's servant among the people,

a channel for the free flowing

of His Spirit, understanding, and love.

I will guide and guard the flock

with disciplined faith and holy integrity.

Following the Biblical pattern of servant leadership,

I will *teach* the fullness of God's Word,

model the fruit of the Spirit,

equip the saints for dynamic discipleship,

preach with compelling compassion,

lead with a clear vision of the abundant life in Christ.

I will give my best to ministry

so that my people can receive the best

from the Master, Jesus Christ!

The Pastor and People in Agreement

Agreement between the Pastor and the people is the foundation for a healthy, vibrant, growing church. Profiles of members and Pastors indicate that there are different personalities and views on how ministry should be performed. God's plan, however, is for the Pastor and the church to come together as a team to perform His will.

The church belongs to the Lord. He has set forth principles on how the Pastor and people are to agree so they can do His work in the church His way. Adopt a Bible-based agreement plan with your Pastor.

Agreement Plan

Agree that **PRAYER** and worship must always be the priorities.

Agree that **PARTNERSHIP** with the Pastor and other members is God's plan for the operation of His church.

Agree that **POSSIBILITIES** to share the love and grace of Christ surround the church, and that seizing these possibilities must be the primary purpose and passion of all the people.

Agree that **PROGRAMS** provide a structure for action, but the needs of people must always be the point of focus.

Agree that **PROMOTION** is a key element in evangelism and outreach, and that this calls for disciplined planning and finances.

Agree that **PERSONNEL** must be enlisted, trained, given responsibility, and honored.

Agree that **PROJECTS** to stimulate ongoing spiritual growth must be constant and challenging.

Agree that **PREACHING** is the primary method of revealing and showing how to apply God's Word, and that sermon preparation requires a major portion of the Pastor's time.

Agree that **POWER** in the church is directed by the Holy Spirit and not by individuals or groups.

Agree that **PRODUCTIVITY** in fulfilling the mission of the church is brought about by oneness of purpose, respect for each other, and accepting accountability for assignments and actions.

How to Be a Difference-Maker Church Member

I believe the goal of every church member is to live a life that makes a difference, to minister with a Pastor that makes a difference, and to belong to a church that makes a difference. Without making a difference, our witness is hollow, God is not honored, and the church fails to reap the harvest fields.

You can be "A Difference-Maker Church Member" by personally saying, "I will." I will be a team player with other church members; I will be a partner in ministry with my Pastor; and I will embrace the five points in the platform of "A Difference-Maker Church Member."

1. MANIFEST a teachable spirit.

If you need need wisdom—if you want to know what God wants you to do—ask Him and He will gladly tell you. "He is generous and enjoys giving to all people, so he will give you wisdom" (James 1:5, *NCV*).

2. DISCOVER your slot in the leadership networking team of the church.

Every day they continued to meet together in the temple courts. They broke bread in their homes and ate together with glad and sincere hearts, praising God and enjoying the favor of all the people. And the Lord added to their number daily those who were being saved (Acts 2:46, 47, *NIV*).

3. RECOGNIZE God's method of fulfilling His plan for the church: the Pastor and the people sharing the responsibilities of ministry.

And Christ gave gifts to people—he made some to be apostles, some to be prophets, some to go and tell the Good News, and some to have the work of caring for and teaching God's people. Christ gave those gifts to prepare God's holy people for the work of serving, to make the body of Christ stronger (Ephesians 4:11, 12, *NCV*).

4. EMBRACE the concept of holding up the Pastor's hands in achieving victory.

But Moses' hands became heavy; so they took a stone and put it under him, and he sat on it. And Aaron and Hur supported his hands, one on one side, and the other on the other side; and his hands were steady. . . . So Joshua defeated Amalek and his people (Exodus 17:12, 13).

5. MAXIMIZE opportunities to excel.

Thank God for letting our Lord Jesus Christ give us the victory! My dear friends, stand firm and don't be shaken. Always keep busy working for the Lord. You know that everything you do for him is worthwhile (1 Corinthians 15:57, 58, *CEV*).

You can be "A Difference-Maker Church Member." You can hold on, hold fast and hold out. You can be a ministry model to others— loving, leading, developing and guiding in power-plus Christian living.

Dynamic Partnership Words for Your Pastor

Ten Dynamic Words – God has called you to equip church members for ministry.

Nine Dynamic Words – You are my shepherd and I will follow you.

Eight Dynamic Words – I believe you have a vision for growth.

Seven Dynamic Words – God has commissioned us to be partners.

Six Dynamic Words – I will pray daily for you.

Five Dynamic Words – I will practice consistent stewardship.

Four Dynamic Words – I will support you.

Three Dynamic Words – Together in mission.

Two Dynamic Words – Share Jesus.

One Dynamic Word – Trust.

Invitation to Interaction

1. Discuss the profiles of different church members. How does it "please God" to have both diversity and unity in His body, the church?

2. Why does God choose to call different types of Pastors to perform His work?

3. Talk about some of the rewards of bringing out the best in other church members and in your Pastor.

4. Review *The Church Member's Creed* and *The Pastor's Creed.*

5. Agreement between the Pastor and the people is the anchor of the local church. Why is this true? How can it be emphasized?

6. List some way you can be a "Difference-Maker Church Member."

CHAPTER FIVE

Pattern of Supporting Your Pastor

OUR CHURCH WILL STAND BY OUR PASTOR

Our church will stand by our Pastor,
United in faith and creed,
Like a mighty army,
Marching forward indeed.

Our church will stand by our Pastor,
Always being a house of prayer,
Watching God's miracles flow,
Filling us with a glorious glow.

Our church will stand by our Pastor,
Mentoring our children and youth,
Showing them what Jesus would do,
Teaching them God's Word is true.

Our church will stand by our Pastor,
A happy family of faith,
Shining with purity and grace,
Triumphantly running the Christian race.

The ABCs of Supporting Your Pastor

A – **ARRANGE** for spectacular appreciation activities.

B – **BECOME** an ambassador for unity and harmony.

C – **COMMUNICATE** good news and success stories.

D – **DREAM** big, bold dreams with your Pastor.

E – **EXHIBIT** a spirit of honor, esteem, high regard.

F – **FLOW** with creative ideas that promote action.

G – **GLOW** with excitement about reaching the lost.

H – **HOLD** up standards of performance excellence.

I – **INSPIRE** others by modeling high loyalty ideals.

J – **JOIN** hands and hearts in responding to God's will.

K – **KINDLE** benevolence and generosity in the church.

L – **LEARN** to give and receive praise gracefully.

M – **MARKET** the virtues of trustworthiness and consistency.

N – **NEUTRALIZE** fault-finding and bias evaluators.

O – **OPEN** doors of understanding rules and responsibilities.

P – **PLAN** for an annual Pastor Appreciation emphasis.

Q – **QUIETLY** network to bolster influence and image.

R – **RESPOND** to challenges to grow and give cheerfully.

S – **STRESS** the Biblical promises of oneness in purpose.

T – **TOUCH** your Pastor through empathy and a warm heart.

U – **UNDERSTAND** the influence of showing respect.

V – **VALUE** coming together as a family to worship.

W – **WORK** for a heavenly crown, not an earthly crown.

X – **EXPRESS** praise to leaders for foresight and steadfastness.

Y – **YELL**, cheer victories, and achieve goals.

Z – **ZEALOUSLY** stand for, with and beside your Pastor.

The Pattern of Supporting Your Pastor

In the first four chapters we built a foundation and framework for joining your Pastor in ministry as a co-worker. Materials and guidelines on how to make the relationship strong have also been given. It may appear that some of the subjects or points have been duplicated. This duplication was intentional. The purpose was to build a case and a cause that cannot be erased or weakened by previous patterns of thinking or present circumstances. This is important in maintaining a vibrant, healthy, growing church.

Chapter 5 will focus on supporting your Pastor, joining him as a partner in ministry and doing the work of the church as a team with him. In addition to the Pastor-member relationship, resources for pinpointing care for church guests, members, church image, and outreach will be set forth. These subjects will be discussed using the theme or method of "understanding" and "how to."

Understanding Your Pastor

The master key in supporting your Pastor is understanding him. We have already talked about his calling and the pressure surrounding his work. Now let's do a quick review and set the stage for outlining ways to be a winning team with him in the work of the local church. The review will be wrapped around four words: Understand what makes your Pastor *tick*, *click*, *kick* and *stick*.

Understand what makes your Pastor TICK.

It's his calling! Look at his calling in Chapter 1. It is personal, binding and irrevocable. It is a six-fold call: a divine call, a direct call, a distinct call, a dynamic call, a delightful call, and a double-honor call. Your Pastor's call is his life; it shapes everything that he does. He can never rest from it. It is always with him, and he has to report to God every day. His call is what makes him **TICK**.

Understand what makes your Pastor CLICK.

It's his gift-mix! Look at profiles of different Pastors in Chapter 4, and understand what drives your Pastor. All of us have spiritual buttons that turn us on in Christian ministry—leading youth, teaching children, visiting the sick, helping the needy, singing in the choir, serving tables, administering care, intercession. Your Pastor has a "turn-on" button, a special gift. Discover what it is, and place a spotlight on it. Maximize his gift. Maximize the gift that makes him **CLICK**.

Understand what makes your Pastor KICK.

It's resistance to God's plan for ministry! God placed a "kick" in your Pastor in order to keep church work pure, urgent and challenging. Stand with your Pastor when it is necessary for him to kick, so he can do it according to God's Word. The people's resistance to God's plan got to Pastor Moses and he said, "Hear now, you rebels! Must we bring water for you out of this rock?" (Numbers 20:10). Unfortunately, he violated God's plan by striking instead of speaking to the rock. Your Pastor must kick against lukewarmness, false teachers and the lack of commitment to God and His church. Stand with him so the church can be united in purpose with him. Resistance to God's plan of ministry makes him **KICK**.

Understand what makes your Pastor STICK.

It's his love for people! God's call on your Pastor's life placed a love for people in his heart that doesn't fade with fatigue, ungratefulness or hardship. He's in it for the long haul. He must give an account to God on how he "fulfilled his ministry." Quitting, turning back, bowing down or giving in are not options. He loves to grow people in the Lord. In recognizing the call to the ministry, he took an oath "to be found faithful." Regardless of pressure, problems, or pitfalls, you can count on him to stick with it. Love for people causes him to **STICK**.

Now take a close look at your Pastor. Carefully survey the gifts God has invested in him for ministry. Using the form *Understanding My Pastor*, record your observations, insights and feelings in these four areas of values. As you observe how God has chosen to endow your Pastor, you will come into a closer relationship with him and will be better prepared to support him in ministry.

Understanding My Pastor
Mapping His Gifts for Ministry

An essential phase of supporting your Pastor is to recognize his strengths, skills, and abilities — what makes him **tick**, **click**, **kick**, and **stick**. This draws you closer to him and helps to pinpoint particular areas for prayer. Use the space in this section to list various strong points in the personality and performance of your Pastor.

I admire my Pastor most for . . .

I appreciate my Pastor because he is . . .

I think my Pastor's greatest strengths are . . .

My Pastor knows how to . . .

Understanding My Nature in Christ

What makes you **tick**, **click**, **kick**, and **stick**? In Chapter 4, profiles of different church members were given. What is your ministry's "hot button?"

Like your Pastor, God has placed certain treasures in your life so you can honor Him and join with your Pastor as a partner in ministry. Place a check mark by the values in the following list that describe you:

_____ Dependable disciple

_____ Happy tither

_____ Bible reader

_____ Fruitful leader

_____ Daily petitioner

_____ Creative worker

_____ Peacekeeper

_____ Programs promoter

_____ Possibility thinker

_____ Community mixer

_____ Effective organizer

_____ Cheerful helper

_____ Personal encourager

_____ Values pusher

_____ Problem solver

_____ Bold discipler

The chances are you have checked several areas that signify gifts. Now determine which gifts are the strongest. Which ones really make you click and tick? Which ones will help your Pastor understand you better? After a time of reflection, complete the *Understanding My Nature in Christ* form.

Understanding My Nature in Christ
Mapping My Gifts for Ministry

Supporting your Pastor is responding to God's call on your life to be a faithful servant in the local church. You must recognize your strengths, skills, and abilities—what makes you **tick**, **click**, **kick** and **stick**—in order to join with your Pastor as a team member in the mission and ministry of the church. Use the space in this section to list the special abilities which God has trusted you to serve with your Pastor:

I am very passionate about:

I feel my greatest strengths are:

Some weak areas in my church life are:

I feel I can be effective in ministry in these areas:

In mapping the Pastor's gifts and your talents, see how they can be brought together to complement each other in ministry. Teamwork and togetherness enable the local church to be whole and healthy. Observe these 20 Togetherness Principles with your Pastor:

__ Respect him	__ Worship with him
__ Trust him	__ Love him
__ Work with him	__ Talk to him
__ Listen to him	__ Honor him
__ Laugh with him	__ Cry with him
__ Witness with him	__ Care for him
__ Minister with him	__ Fellowship with him
__ Stand with him	__ Appreciate him
__ Pray with him	__ Celebrate with him
__ Believe with him	__ Build with him

As you practice these principles, your church life will have a bright, fulfilling luster and glow. God's plan—Pastor and people as a team—always produces harmony and happiness in the church family.

Praying for Your Pastor

One of the greatest things you can do as a partner with your Pastor is to pray for him. This is the foundation for partnership. It is keeping the faith of the saints. This is the path to follow for securing the flow of God's grace on the church. In this section we present the power of prayer for your Pastor, the principles involved in praying for him and proven programs that help establish consistent and fruitful prayer.

> "Prayer for the Pastor brings the
> church together as God's
> team to provide hope for the world."

When You Pray for Your Pastor

♦ It *reveals* **AFFIRMATION** – You are pro-pastor and believe he is called and anointed by God.

♦ It *shows* **AGREEMENT** – You are united with him in fulfilling the mission of the church.

♦ It *builds* **ATTITUDE** – You are positive in responding to opportunities to serve and relate.

♦ It *denotes* **ADVENTURE** – You are ready to respond to God's plan for the church.

♦ It *fosters* **ADVANCEMENT** – You are open to change and to be accountable for performing ministry.

A great picture of the power of prayer by the church for their Pastor is found in Acts 12:1-17. Peter was the Pastor of a house church. He was placed in prison by Herod because of the effectiveness of his ministry. "But constant prayer was offered to God for him by the church" (v. 5).

The church was praying fervently—stretching intercessory muscles; praying specifically—for its Pastor; praying collectively—the entire congregation; and praying unceasingly—around the clock. As the church prayed for its Pastor, we know that four dynamic things happened:

1. **There Was a Divine Visitation**—God sent an angel to guide him (v. 7).

2. **There Was Disbursement of Darkness**—"A light shone in the prison" (v. 7).

3. **There Was Deliverance From Obstacles**—"His chains fell off his hands" (v. 7).

4. **A Doorway Was Opened**—"The iron gate that leads to the city . . . opened to them of its own accord" (v. 10). Then Peter shared with his people "how the Lord had brought him out of the prison" as they prayed for him (v. 17).

This is a remarkable illustration of what God does when the church prays for its Pastor. God visits the church with divine manifestations.

He gives liberty and removes barriers. He opens the gates to the city for the church to walk through and impact city government, businesses, schools and communities.

When a church prays for its Pastor, the Holy Spirit brings the spirit of church members together with their Pastor in affirmation and affirmative action. Prayer still changes things—churches, Pastors, people.

The church must commit to praying for its Pastor. The church must commit to . . .

> **EXCELLENCE** in prayer — *Priority.*
>
> **ELEGANCE** in prayer — *Devotion.*
>
> **ENDURANCE** in prayer — *Consistency.*
>
> **ENJOYMENT** in prayer — *Fellowship.*

Also, consistent prayer should be made for the Pastor's family. Not only the Pastor but his entire family must be under the covering of the church.

Praying for Your Pastor's Family

1. **PRAY** that his family will be protected from unrealistic expectations and unfair comparisons by church members.

2. **PRAY** that his companion will find identity, significance, and fulfillment in the pursuit of a personal career and the use of personal spiritual gifts.

3. **PRAY** that his family will be bound together in love for each other and the church would respect their right for seasons of privacy.

4. **PRAY** that his children will have good experiences in church relationships, at school, and in social activities.

5. **PRAY** that his home life will provide an environment for relaxation, rejuvenation, interaction, and supportive companionship.

Positive Prayer Plans for Your Pastor

Organize *a Pastor's Prayer Partners Program.*

The size of this group will depend on the size of your church. It can be large or small. Partners form a prayer force to intercede for the Pastor every day. A guidebook can be ordered from the *Church of God Department of Lay Ministries, PO Box 2430, Cleveland, TN 37320-2430.* The team comes together monthly for instructions and intercession, holds an annual Partners Prayer Retreat, designates individuals to pray with the Pastor on Sunday mornings, and checks with the Pastor about personal and church needs. The prayer team bonds with the Pastor, and both parties are blessed with spiritual blessings.

Conduct *a Prayer for the Pastor Evening Service.*

The recommended time for this is at the beginning of the year on a Sunday evening. It is somewhat like a solemn assembly. The program is structured but there is free flowing expression and intercession. The order of the service would include scripture readings on the ministry of the church, the position and work of the Pastor, vision for discipleship and outreach, protection for the Pastor's family, and harmony and unity among church members. There would be individual and corporate prayer throughout the program. Motivational music would also be an essential element in creating a spirit of prayer.

Sponsor *a Men's Prayer Breakfast.*

At least once a year the men of the church should come together for a Prayer Breakfast to support and encourage their Pastor. This is always a special time for both the men and the Pastor. It breeds a closeness and a renewed loyalty to each other. The men are able to express their prayer support, and the Pastor is able to respond in an open and transparent way. The physical laying on of hands by the men transmits spiritual energy and encouragement to the Pastor.

Promote *Prayer for the Pastor Among Church Members.*

There should be a regular emphasis on praying for the Pastor. This can be done in several different ways: items in the church bulletin, a week of prayer for the Pastor, a personal prayer Biblemark, prayer coin, imprinted items to display in homes. Remember the prayer illustration from Acts 12:5 — "But constant prayer was offered to God for [its Pastor] by the church."

Form an *Intercessors Prayer Group.*

Intercessors are a special group of individuals who feel called to a ministry of prayer. They actually pray in a special location during the service for God to bless the music, the worship, and the preaching of the Word. They often meet during the week to pray for the Pastor as he studies, and to bring the ministries of the church before the Lord.

Change your outlook about the ministry of your Pastor through prayer, and you will change your involvement and influence in the ministry of the church.

Praying for Your Pastor and Church

A Daily Guide Through the New Testament

Every church member should have a copy of this book. It provides an exciting journey through the New Testament as the Holy Spirit guides you in partnering with your heavenly Father, your Pastor, and church members in God-honoring worship, in joyfully reaping the harvest, and in coming together for building, enriching, and supportive fellowship.

ORDER FROM: *The Pastor and the People,* Floyd D. Carey, 2800 Metropolitan Way, Birmingham, AL 35243

How to Put a PUNCH in Praying for Your Pastor

When you consider the word *punch*, you most likely will associate it with a strong blow with a fist. However, it can also be identified with intensity and powerful words in a speech or conversation. When you pray for your Pastor, put "punch" in your words. Let them pack meaning. Observe the following pattern built around the letters in the word *PUNCH*.

P – **PARTNER** with the Holy Spirit in praying for your Pastor. Ask the Holy Spirit to witness through you and reveal the soul needs of your Pastor and how you can help meet them.

U – **UNITE** with the vision of your Pastor as you pray for Him. Ask God to let you feel the burden, embrace the vision, and equip you to stand shoulder to shoulder with your Pastor.

N – **NURTURE** congregational harmony in your petitions. Pray for a spirit of togetherness, unified teamwork, and cheerful coordination to cover the entire congregation.

C – **CONDITION** your mind to pray blessings on your Pastor. Fill your minds with scriptures of power, promises, and possibilities. Pray blessings on your Pastor.

H – **HONOR** God's promises for your pastor and church as you pray. Ask God to affirm His promises to overshadow the life of your Pastor and to move the church forward.

"Remember your leaders, who spoke the word of God to you. Consider the outcome of their way of life and imitate their faith" (Hebrews 13:7, *NIV*).

How to Honor Your Pastor

You honor your Pastor by standing beside him and by joining him in ministry as a partner. This entire book is about honoring God and His selection of your Pastor as a shepherd, soldier and servant-leader. In every chapter there are covenants, pledges and uniting Pastor and people together as co-workers—one dream, one team and one in spirit. You can do personal things that will honor your Pastor and bring you closer to him in love and ministry. Look at these special areas.

PASTOR APPRECIATION/ANNIVERSARY SUNDAY

At least once a year the local church should sponsor a Pastor Appreciation Sunday or a special event. Some churches do this on Anniversary Sunday. This is a time to recall God's blessings during the past year, to spotlight the fruit of the Pastor's ministry, and to create a deep spirit of thankfulness among the people.

The Church of God Department of Lay Ministries produces a Pastor Appreciation program every year. It features a compelling theme, guidelines and support materials. The ideas are current and refreshing, and the support items are cost-friendly. Contact: Department of Lay Ministries, PO Box 2430, Cleveland, TN 37320-2430.

One Pastor Appreciation event becoming popular is a Pastor Appreciation Family Night Festival. The program includes a meal, displays of church heritage, skits, expressions of appreciation from children, youth and adults, video of church/Pastor activities, and uplifting fellowship. This event breeds a great respect and love for the church, the Pastor, and for each other.

Ways to Honor and Bless Your Pastor

1. Affirm the Pastor's commitment for change to increase worship involvement and outreach intensity.
2. Agree with him for developing quality and excellence in ministry.
3. Ask friends to attend church with you.
4. Ask the mayor to proclaim a Pastor Appreciation Day in the city.
5. Ask the Pastor, "How can I help you?"

6. Attend church regularly.
7. Back him in challenging the status quo.
8. Be a cheerleader for the Pastor.
9. Be a good follower.
10. Be a good listener; let his sermons sink deep.
11. Aggressively form a personal relationship with your Pastor.
12. Be available and willing to listen to his plans for effectiveness and growth.
13. Be aware of the demands on his time.
14. Be consistent in your witness and work in the church.
15. Believe with him that God wants to do "new things" in the church.
16. Buy into the Pastor's vision; accept ownership.
17. Call him up and convey love and respect for his ministry.
18. Compliment him for timely and compassion-driven sermons.
19. Defend the Pastor against fault-findings and criticisms.
20. Display a teachable spirit; let the Pastor disciple you.
21. Don't ever say, "We've never done it that way before."
22. Embrace his focus on discipleship training.
23. Encourage him with words and works.
24. Encourage the Pastor's wife to be her own person.
25. Feature a write-up in the local newspaper about the ministry of the Pastor.
26. Furnish him with fishing equipment and encourage him to get away from strain and stress.
27. Give him frequent flyer tickets for a special trip.
28. Give him Scriptural submission according to Hebrews 13:17.
29. Give the Pastor a cost-of-living increase in salary each year.
30. Have confidence in the Pastor's motives and abilities.
31. Help form a Pastoral Concerns Team to provide for the needs of the Pastor and his family.
32. Help create and champion visionary plans for church growth.
33. Help the congregation establish privacy boundaries. Provide the Pastor with time to be alone with God and with his family.
34. Hold up his hands as he leads the flock.

35. Jump in and assist him on behind-the-scene projects.
36. Let him make mistakes.
37. Let the Pastor dream and be creative.
38. Listen to him; let him share his story.
39. Listen to the Pastor's long-range goals and plans.
40. Look for ways to make the Pastor look and feel good.
41. Make it known you are a "Pastor person."
42. Make sure he has a day off each week.
43. Make sure he has adequate health care coverage.
44. Organize a Pastor's Prayer Partners Ministry.
45. Participate in Pastor Appreciation activities.
46. Pay your tithes consistently.
47. Plan a church appreciation banquet for the Pastor.
48. Pray for the Pastor and his family by name every day.
49. Provide him with retirement benefits and reputable counsel.
50. Refrain from saying, "That will cost too much!"
51. Relay to him how a sermon blessed your life.
52. Say to him often, "Pastor, I'm praying for you!"
53. Say to the Pastor, "I'm with you. You can count on me!"
54. Send the Pastor a humorous card — brighten his day.
55. Share good news with him.
56. Show the community love in action by providing for and supporting the Pastor.
57. Sing "Bind Us Together in Love" with him.
58. Stand by him when he is in the line of fire.
59. Stand up for his programs.
60. Stick with him when you don't understand his reasoning and approach.
61. Support the Pastor with action, affirmation and accountability.
62. Support the Pastor with your time, talents, tithes and treasures.
63. Take notes while he preaches.
64. Talk to him; build a relationship of teamwork.
65. Teach your children to respect him.

66. Tell him you willingly submit to his leadership and teaching.
67. Trust the decisions of the Pastor.
68. Understand the "glass house" syndrome; encourage the Pastor's children.
69. Volunteer to assist in special projects and activities.
70. Write the Pastor a letter and express love and appreciation for his integrity and leadership.

How to Restrict Intrusions and Increase Your Pastor's Effectiveness

To be effective in the demands placed on him, your Pastor must do three things: 1) He must be sensitive to God; 2) He must have seasons of solitude; and 3) He must screen interruptions. All three are essential.

Your Pastor must be sensitive to the voice of God. He must receive a message from God each week for the people. This requires solitude, being alone with God. This also calls for screening. The process of screening means not responding to some things in order to do the main thing—to spend time with God and His Word. This calls for using staff members, elders and church members to do the work of ministry.

There are several ways you can help in restricting intrusions:

Affirm the ministry of elders. They rest under the covering/anointing of the Pastor. Call elders and let them anoint with oil, pray for the sick, listen to problems, and give spiritual counsel.

Understand that less than 10 percent of the people require 90 percent of the Pastor's time. Help direct these individuals to other sources of encouragement. Don't let every contact with the Pastor at church be a crisis, a counseling session, a confession, or a critical observation. Give him free time to minister and speak to all of the people.

Along with the church staff, become a minister. Let the Pastor teach and equip, and let all of us do the work of ministry. When this pattern was followed in Acts 6:1-7, "The word of God spread, and the number of the disciples multiplied greatly" (v. 7). God has called us all to do the work of ministry.

The heavy demands placed on your Pastor strain and stretch him. That is why it is so important to support him. When Solomon built the temple, he needed three things—wisdom, wealth and workers. Your Pastor needs these same three things. Pray that God will give him wisdom, and that He will use you to supply wealth and to be a worker.

How to Keep Your Pastor's Sermons Stored in Your Memory

Paul told the believers at Corinth that he preached to them what he had received, that "Christ died for our sins according to the Scriptures" (1 Corinthians 15:3). He was saying, *I preached God's Word to you so keep it stored in your memory; it is vital, life-giving, life-directing.*

Your Pastor will preach more than 100 sermons every year. They will include a wide range of subjects—Bible doctrine, spiritual devotion, life-style dedication, and personal development. His sermons are a wealth of material, a library for successful, God-honoring, Christ-exalting and Spirit-powered living. Don't just sit, shout or sleep through sermons; soak them up. Store them in your memory. Build a structure for sermons so they can stay with you and become a part of your Christian journey. Here are four steps of action to help you listen to a sermon.

LOOK at your Pastor while he is preaching. Do not be distracted by looking around, talking to a person beside you or cuddling a baby. You can miss the framework and flow of a sermon quickly. Looking at your Pastor helps to focus on both the content and the intent of the message. It helps you feel what he is saying, and helps block out memory-blurring thoughts.

LISTEN for the connecting points of the sermon. At the beginning of the message, try to determine what the Pastor wants you to know, to feel, to do and to remember. Paint a picture in your mind of the title of the sermon. Connect the title to the main points, to stories and illustrations. Develop a listening mind-set. Flow and glow with the sermon.

LABEL each sermon. Take notes on Sunday morning and you will have 52 sermon titles at the end of the year. The main points of each sermon can be stored in your memory. Arrange the sermon topics under three main headings or points. If possible, confine your notes to one page. Survey the page of notes and let the title, points and stories find a place in your memory through identification and association.

LEARN and **LIVE** the sermon. Under "Listen" you tried to ascertain what the Pastor wanted you to know, to feel, to do and to remember. At the conclusion of the sermon, ask: What did I learn? What did I experience? What do I need to do? What do I need to store in my memory? This will guide you in living out the sermon in daily life and in developing as a strong, mature person in Christ. As you store sermons in your memory, your soul becomes "a library for Christ."

Understanding the Elements of Lay and Pastoral Leadership

Church attendance and agreeing with Great Commission goals is just the beginning of discipleship responsibilities. There must be leadership teamwork—the laity and the Pastor coming together to make church growth happen. These 10 elements bring the laity and the Pastor together in developing and demonstrating leadership in the Church.

Listening to the voice of God, the instructions of the Pastor, and the requests of church members.

Empowering workers to perform with creativity without being second-guessed or placed in a mold.

Advancing the mission of the church through compassion-centered ministries that touch people at their point of need.

Developing potential ministry leaders through mentoring, training, and service opportunities.

Enlarging the vision of followers by serving as a role model and by displaying drive and determination.

Responding to challenges to expand church programs and upgrade methods of making the church family stronger.

Showing respect for each member of the church family and an understanding of their needs.

Helping church members find their place in the body of Christ and in the utilization of their spiritual gifts for ministry.

Initiating new approaches to ministry that increase effectiveness, efficiency, and enthusiasm.

Providing avenues for evaluation of church ministries, personal performance, training, and recognition for achievements.

Understanding God's Plan of Tithing and Giving

Giving patterns of the average American church member were documented in a Gallup Poll. A little more than 17 percent said they tithed, but only three percent actually did. Ninety-one percent told the pollsters they made more money than ever, yet 40 percent confessed they gave the church nothing last year. To be loyal to the church and Pastor, and especially to Jesus Christ, requires regular tithing.

TITHING IS GOD'S PLAN FOR FINANCING HIS WORK

♦ Abraham COMMENCED the practice of tithing (Genesis 14:18-20; Hebrews 7:4-9).

♦ Moses COMMANDED the principle of tithing (Leviticus 27:30; Deuteronomy 14:22).

♦ Hezekiah CONFIRMED the blessings of tithing (2 Chronicles 31:2-10).

♦ Nehemiah CENSURED the neglect of tithing (Nehemiah 13:10-14).

◆ Malachi CONFIRMED the curses of God for neglecting to tithe (Malachi 3:8-12).

◆ Jesus COMMENDED even the uncommitted for tithing (Matthew 23:23).

◆ Paul urges us to CONTINUE the Biblical principle of tithing (1 Corinthians 16:2; 2 Corinthians 8:12).

TITHING DENOTES LOVE AND LOYALTY

◆ "If you give what you do not need, it isn't giving." *Mother Teresa*

◆ "God judges what we give by what we keep." *George Mueller*

◆ "I have tried to keep things in my hands and lost them all, but what I have given into God's hands I still possess." *Martin Luther*

YOU NEED TO TITHE BECAUSE:

◆ Tithing motivates the believer to greater faithfulness. It is the starting point for giving. Tithing releases God's financial blessings in an unbelievable way. He has promised to open the "floodgates of heaven" to faithful tithers (Malachi 3:10, *NIV*).

◆ Tithing expands the work of the Kingdom of God. It has the potential for changing the spending habits of believers.

◆ Tithing reflects our attitude toward the church and toward God. It is a memory peg constantly reminding us of the priority of God in all we are, all we have, and all we do. Jesus said, "If your profits are in heaven your heart will be there too" (Matthew 6:21, *TLB*).

TITHING ENABLES THE LOCAL CHURCH TO FULFILL ITS MISSION

◆ Responsible stewardship has the dynamic potential to do many wonderful things.

◆ Responsible stewardship turns temporary commodities (money) into eternal things.

- Responsible stewardship has a way of keeping us from being materialistic and selfish.

- Responsible stewardship will help us to learn to deepen our trust in God.

- Responsible stewardship provides us with opportunities to show our gratitude to God.

WHERE AND TO WHOM SHOULD A BELIEVER TITHE?

The word *tithe* means "a tenth," and the Bible makes it clear that it belongs to the Lord. Where, or to whom, should a believer tithe?

- Seek the place where the Lord your God chooses . . . to put His name for His dwelling place; and there you shall go. There you shall take your . . . tithes . . . your freewill offerings (Deuteronomy 12:5, 6).

- Hezekiah commanded them to prepare rooms in the house of the Lord. . . . Then they faithfully brought in the offerings, the tithes (2 Chronicles 31:11, 12).

- Bring the tithes . . . to the Levites . . . to the house of our God, to the rooms of the storehouse (Nehemiah 10:37, 38).

- "Bring all the tithes into the storehouse, that there may be food in My house, and try Me now in this," says the Lord of hosts, "if I will not open for you the windows of heaven and pour out for you such blessing that there will not be room enough to receive it. And I will rebuke the devourer for your sakes, so that he will not destroy the fruit of your ground, nor shall the vine fail to bear fruit for you in the field," says the Lord of hosts (Malachi 3:10, 11).

The local church is the "house of the Lord," the "storehouse" where He has "put His name."

Understanding God-Honoring Compensation for Your Pastor

The Bible is clear about providing for your Pastor, "[Pastors] who direct the affairs of the church well are worthy of double honor, especially those whose work is preaching and teaching" (1 Timothy 5:17, *NIV*). "Double Honor" calls for *Respect* and *Remuneration*.

Respect for the Pastor's calling and position. *Respect* for his preaching and teaching. *Respect* for his oversight and leadership.

Remuneration for the Pastor by displaying a positive, receptive spirit. *Remuneration* by a thankful attitude for his steadfast, totally devoted commitment to nurture and develop disciples. *Remuneration* in the form of a compensation package that recognizes his needs, the needs of his family, and the need to be financially stable and secure.

The story of the Shunammite woman and Elisha depicts a holy stance in honoring and providing for the man of God. Read the story in 2 Kings 4:8-37. Let us trace three action steps of this "notable" (v. 8) woman:

Step One – She recognized his credentials: "I know that this is a holy man of God" (v. 9).

Step Two – She recognized his need for proper housing "Let us make a[n] . . . upper room" (v. 10).

Step Three – She recognized his need for comfort and convenience, "Let us put a bed for him there, and a table and a chair and a lampstand; so . . . whenever he comes to us, he can turn in there" (v. 10).

The Shunammite woman did not try to skimp or save. She made sure he was given a total compensation package. Because she blessed her Pastor, she was blessed. Let us trace three areas of blessings.

Area One — She was blessed with family happiness; "'About this time next year you shall embrace a son. . . .' The woman conceived, and bore a son" (vv. 16, 17).

Area Two – She was blessed with family wholeness and healing. The child grew. One day he said to his father; "My head, my head!" (v. 19). He sat on his mother's knees until noon, and then died. "She went up and laid him on the bed of the man of God" (v. 21). Elisha was called, he prayed for the child, God raised him up . . . he was presented to his mother (vv. 18-37).

Area Three – She was protected from famine, and she had her property restored;"Then Elisha spoke to the woman . . . '[T]he Lord has called for a famine. . . .' She went . . . and dwelt in the land of the Philistines seven years" (8:1, 2). After seven years she returned home. "The king appointed a certain officer for her, saying, 'Restore all that was hers, and the proceeds of the fields from the day that she left the land until now'" (v. 6).

This Biblical story shows the impact of caring for the Pastor/ shepherd. It demonstrates significance and fulfillment, care and healing, security and prosperity. These provisions are offered today in the caring process of your Pastor. The Pastor is blessed, the church is blessed and the congregation is blessed.

The Pastor is relieved of the strain of financial pressure. This makes him more effective and productive. The church is blessed by your generosity: "It is possible to give away and become richer! It is also possible to hold on too tightly and lose everything. Yes, the liberal man shall be rich! By watering others, he waters himself" (Proverbs 11:24, 25, *TLB*).

The congregation that shares partnership with its Pastor and avoids frequent pastoral transitions is doubly blessed. "Let him who is taught the word share in all good things with him who teaches" (Galatians 6:6).

A Pastor's Compensation Package

When looking at providing for your Pastor, remember the words of Christ, "Give, and it will be given to you … for by your standard of measure, it will be measured to you in return" (Luke 6:38, *NASB*). Keep in mind the life and ministry of a Pastor is different. Avoid comparing his work and salary with other churches and professions. Remember, he must set the example in both spiritual commitment and in financial giving. He lives a self-emptying life of giving his all to ministry. This is why a majority of Pastors are not prepared for retirement. Carefully consider 10 elements in providing security for your Pastor.

Provide:

1. Salary based on worth and experience.
2. Medical needs and life insurance.
3. Expense account for continuing education and ministry-related hospitality.
4. Housing allowance or furnished church parsonage.
5. Car and traveling allowance.
6. Cost-of-living adjustments in salary.
7. Vacation and sabbatical considerations.
8. Christmas or end-of-year bonus.
9. Framework for a secure retirement.
10. Cheerful spirit toward the compensation package: "God loves a cheerful [giving church]" (2 Corinthians 9:7).

A giving church will be a growing church. A receiving Pastor will be a contented, responsible Pastor. An understanding congregation will be a mature, motivated congregation honoring God and advancing His Kingdom.

When Your Pastor Leaves

When a Pastor leaves a church for another place of ministry, it is never easy for the congregation or the departing minister. Sometimes the congregation feels disappointed or betrayed; sometimes it is the departing Pastor who feels betrayed. As a member of the congregation, however, you can be influential in helping the church do the ethical and right thing. Whether the Pastor leaves on friendly terms or under fire, you owe him respect and a proper send-off.

♦ Be sensitive to the importance of what is taking place. No matter how long a Pastor has served, it is a time of crisis for him.

He has formed many relationships, and he may have family who lives nearby.

♦ Cutting ties and leaving friends is never easy on the Pastor's spouse. Packing, moving away from familiar things—doctors, shopping places, and many other familiar conveniences—can be traumatic.

♦ For the children this is especially true. They are leaving friends, changing schools, sometimes leaving jobs. Children do not understand all the things happening in their parents' lives, and this can be a time of confusion for them.

♦ The Pastor realizes, sometimes with a jolt, that he will be leaving people he has developed and nurtured in the Christian faith. His shepherd-heart often hurts with the thought of what is taking place.

♦ The Pastor is faced with the expenses of moving. Sometimes this involves the selling of furniture, a house, or other conveniences he may not be able to take to his new place of residence.

♦ Honor the Pastor who is leaving by giving him a going-away banquet, a party, or an all-church meal. Present him with a sizeable cash gift and a plaque that documents and honors his time spent in ministry with you. Allow the congregation to present the Pastor and his family with gifts of gratitude for his service.

♦ Write notes of encouragement. Arrange for meals as they pack. Help clean, load furniture, and so forth.

♦ Instead of this being a heartbreaking event, see it as a wonderful opportunity to bless the Pastor you love in special ways and make him feel his work is appreciated. Make it easy for the family. Express your love, respect and appreciation for them.

When a New Pastor Arrives

Moving to a new location, unpacking in a strange environment, and getting adjusted to new surroundings is equally difficult. When a new Pastor comes, there are many things you and other leaders can do to make the transition as smooth and painless as possible.

BEFORE THE NEW PASTOR ARRIVES

◆   When the appointment is officially announced to the congregation, the church leaders should contact the new Pastor immediately, and welcome him and his family to the church.

◆   Put together a packet of information about your community. This could be sent in advance, or it can be waiting at the parsonage when he arrives. The packet might include a city map, your church directory and information about doctors, dentists, schools, shopping malls, restaurants and utility companies.

◆   As a nice welcoming gift from the church, consider giving the new Pastor a gift certificate to a local grocery store or other shop. Send him a subscription to the local newspaper.

SPRUCE UP THE PARSONAGE

◆   Appoint a person or committee to make sure the parsonage is clean and ready for the new Pastor and his family. Paint and make any repairs needed before the new Pastor arrives.

◆   If you are painting or redecorating, consider letting the new family choose the colors or new pieces of furniture because they will be living with it.

◆   Make sure all of the utilities are turned on and in good working order. Don't change the parsonage telephone number unless it is necessary or the new Pastor requests it.

◆   Have the lawn mowed and neatly trimmed when the new Pastor arrives.

REFURBISH THE CHURCH OFFICE

◆   This is a good time to redecorate the church office. Also, it is an excellent time to upgrade some of the office equipment, such as the copier, and so forth.

◆   Check with the new Pastor to see if he will need a computer, printer, e-mail service, cell phone, and so forth.

◆   Leave a hymnal in the office with a list of the favorite hymns of the congregation.

WELCOME THE NEW PASTOR ON MOVING DAY

♦ Assign church members to greet and welcome the new Pastor and family as they arrive at the parsonage or the place where they will live.

♦ When the unloading is complete, only stay around and help with unpacking boxes if invited.

♦ If possible, ask a few members to bring a casserole or bucket of takeout chicken to the parsonage for the first few days. Make it easier for the member and the Pastor by delivering food in disposable containers

♦ Plan a churchwide event, like a reception or ice cream social.

♦ Consider a "pounding" where members bring a pound of sugar, flour or other staples to stock the parsonage pantry.

WELCOME THE ENTIRE FAMILY

♦ Find out the ages of the children, and make a list of church kids who are the same age or go to the same school.

♦ Inquire discreetly and see if the new Pastor is caring for an elderly parent. Send them cards, flowers, tapes, and so forth; and welcome them to the congregation.

♦ Plan a party for family members. Keep it light and funny. Plan separate events for kids and spouse.

♦ If the Pastor has young children, give his wife a list of possible babysitters.

♦ Make the transition easier for the "preacher's kids" by inviting the children home to socialize with your children or grandchildren.

INTRODUCE THE NEW PASTOR TO THE TOWN

♦ Plan a get-acquainted, driving tour of the community to show the Pastor and family local businesses, schools, landmarks, and interesting sights.

♦ Take the new Pastor around town and introduce him to community leaders and the staff at the hospital(s).

♦ Run an ad or news article in the local newspaper announcing the arrival of the new Pastor.

♦ Prepare a community map, noting where church members live.

♦ Urge various groups at your church to invite the new Pastor to their favorite restaurant for a get-acquainted session.

BE OPEN, KIND, FAIR AND PATIENT

♦ Allow the new Pastor to set his own pace. Don't expect the Pastor to be at dozens of places and events in his first few days on the job.

♦ Avoid making comparisons between the new Pastor and former ones. Never be guilty of saying, "Pastor So-and-So would never have done it that way."

♦ Be open to new ideas and new ways of doing things. Be responsive when you come to church. Nurture a receptive heart and an open mind.

♦ Be aware of rules of Pastoral etiquette. Use wisdom in inviting the former Pastor to return to conduct funerals or weddings.

♦ Have the Administrative Board of Elders or the Pastor's Council to prepare a written "state of the church" report for the new Pastor. Tell about the plans made at the beginning of the year and where the church stands in completing those plans and programs. Include a list of immediate needs for the remainder of the year.

When Your Pastor Retires

When your Pastor retires, it represents his entire lifetime of ministry. He may have been at your church five years, 10 years or 30 years. However long his tenure, you should remember to include his entire lifetime of ministry in the retirement plans.

♦ Arrange several retirement activities, including banquets and receptions. Try to include as many of his entire extended family as possible in the festivities.

♦ Present the retiring Pastor with an attractively designed award plaque connoting his ministry and achievements.

◆   Present him with meaningful and significant financial gifts.

◆   Arrange for the local newspaper to run a feature about him and his ministry.

◆   Invite the friends of the retiring Pastor from other churches where he has served. Ask for letters and expressions from those who cannot come. Invite some to tell personal experiences that will inspire the congregation.

◆   Plan a big Sunday celebration with guest speakers, reading of expressions, and video story of the retiring Pastor's ministry.

◆   Take advantage of the opportunity to honor the man of God for a lifetime of service. In honoring the man of God, you are honoring not only the work of God, but you are honoring God Himself!

The Value of Pledges, Proclamations, and Covenants

We conclude this chapter with four *Stand By Your Pastor* personal affirmations. These affirmations focus on spiritual surrender, personal stretching and church service. Study the implications of each; then personalize them and make them a part of your commitment to Christ and the church.

Excellence in Ministry Personal Pledge. We all agree God deserves our best in staying close to Him, in becoming spiritually mature, and in serving with compassion and authority. Study the Commitment to Excellence Pledge, sign it, and strive to practice it every day.

Pledging Loyalty to Your Pastor. Loyalty is the base for honoring God and His appointed shepherd. Learn the meaning of how loyalty looks, how it behaves and how it impacts the effectiveness of the church.

Proclamation of Trust and Honor. This is a pledge by the church to the Pastor. It should be read during a study session, in a worship service, and posted in the church lobby.

My Covenant With My Pastor. Contentment in the church is built around your relationship with your Pastor. Determine to stand with him and by him. The "My Covenant" will serve as a daily reminder and guide.

"The local church is the hope of the world." As the Pastor and the People come together as a team, partners in ministry, the impact of the church in the community will be magnified and the Kingdom of God will be advanced.

Excellence in Ministry
Personal Pledge

I am committed to excellence . . .

In **purity** of worship and witness.

In **prayer** and diligent study.

In **praise** and daily thanksgiving.

In **purpose** and ministry objectives.

In **personal** conduct and relationships.

In **positive** role-modeling and mentoring.

In **performance** goals and lifestyle.

In **productivity** and consistent vision.

In **partnership** and teamwork loyalty.

In **promoting** and honoring excellence.

Signed _____

Pledging Loyalty to Your Pastor
— God's Plan for His Church —

True allegiance to God and His called shepherd, your Pastor, is manifested in loyalty. Just as His plan for the church cannot be fulfilled without binding loyalty to Him—heart, mind, soul and body, so His plan for the Pastor and people of the church cannot be achieved without love-based, binding loyalty, teamwork and growth in Christ-likeness. The loyalty plan is outlined in the word *loyalty*:

L – **Loving** relationship based on God's grace and faithfulness.

O – **Ordered** lifestyle of mixing Scriptural belief with daily behavior.

Y – **Yielded** to God's order of leadership and partnership in the church.

A – **Attentive** to church responsibilities and consistent performance.

L – **Learning** and growing into a mature, disciplined follower of Christ.

T – **Together** with the Pastor in fulfilling the mission of the church.

Y – **Yearning** to reach, witness, enlist, and establish the unchurched.

We the People of the Local Church

In Appreciation and Respect
Proclaim Trust and Honor

To Our Beloved Pastor

We Pledge to you **LIBERTY** – the opportunity to minister with freedom among us, with us, and through us to fulfill God's call on your life and God's will for our church.

We Pledge to you **JUSTICE** – to join you in ministry, to demonstrate fairness, uprightness, and honesty, and to be even-tempered and spiritually sensitive in responsibilities and relationships.

We Pledge to you **KINDNESS** – a steady flow of love that reflects respect for your sacrificial work, your visionary leadership, and your need for financial security, relaxation, and time with your family.

We Pledge to you **SOLID SUPPORT** – praying daily for God's anointing and guidance on your life and showing faithfulness in church attendance, personal soulwinning, financial stewardship, and growth in discipleship.

My Covenant Commitment
With My Pastor

Understanding that it is God's plan for the Pastor and the People to come together as Partners, co-workers in the mission and ministries of the local church, I covenant:

- ◆ To **SUPPORT** him with an attitude of congeniality, openness, and cooperation.

- ◆ To **STRENGTHEN** him with a caring spirit of trust, loyalty, and dependability.

- ◆ To **STAND** with him in confidence for visionary planning and consistent performance.

- ◆ To **SAFEGUARD** him with authority against pastoral fatigue and unfounded criticism.

- ◆ To **SALUTE** him in honor for compassionate leadership and Kingdom achievements.

Signed _____

Invitation to Interaction

1. How can your Pastor be supported when he has to "kick" because of compromise, confusion, or lack of commitment?

2. Share what you are passionate about. How can your gifts advance church outreach?

3. What programs can be created to support your Pastor in daily prayer?

4. Discuss the benefits of honoring your Pastor.

5. Why is excellence in ministry God's standard?

6. In what ways can you display loyalty to your church and Pastor?

Resource Material

This material can be used in planning outreach programs, supporting your Pastor in projects and in teaching about church responsibilities.

Reasons People Leave a Local Church

Look closely at your church and other churches. Individuals and families do leave. Why? There are reasons and we must honestly and prayerfully analyze them. We must look at them, learn from them, and provide leadership to correct them.

People leave a church for seven prominent reasons. As we consider each one, evaluate how it relates to your church, and list ways to improve or correct the situation:

1. Celebration   2. Children   3. Community
4. Convenience   5. Controversy   6. Currency
                      7. Commitment

1. CELEBRATION

People attend church to experience God. This encompasses many facets of ministry and personal preferences. The core of experiencing God is the worship service — praise, prayer and preaching. Praise is personally honoring God, prayer is feeling or touching God, and preaching is receiving guidance from God's Word.

There can be too much or not enough in any of the three areas of worship: Not comfortable with style or the changing of styles, not enough freedom of expression, too much freedom, standing too long, being seated too long, service length too long, music and songs too traditional, too contemporary, too loud, not enough variety. Not enough time allowed for personal involvement. The preaching is too shallow (I'm not being fed), too deep (over my head), too long (doesn't know when to quit), not relevant (content doesn't address everyday life).

A closer look – Three steps to action

Accept the character of your church—who you are and how you worship with praise, prayer and preaching. Like attracts like.

Survey the thinking and feelings of your people. Small changes can produce big results.

Utilize a worship team approach in planning worship services. It is easy for one or two people to ignore weaknesses and settle into a pattern of sameness.

2. CHILDREN

Three questions a person asks before identifying with a church are: Will you accept me like I am? What will you provide for my children? Will you offer me a meaningful place of involvement? As you can see, provision for children is the number two reason a family attends a church, and the number two reason a family leaves a church. Children are the present and future of a local church. A ministry to children involves teaching, togetherness and time.

There must be balance between these ingredients. Parents want their children to learn the Bible, to grow spiritually and to form relationships. This requires age-level curriculum, properly equipped and motivated workers, and a priority focus on training. Children must have friends that reach beyond Sunday morning. If they feel isolated, they will complain and ask if they can go to another church with school friends.

Time is a crucial factor. If church services are too long, and children have to stay in Sunday school and Children's Church for an extended period of time, the parents, children and teachers feel tired, off schedule and unfulfilled.

A closer look—Three steps to action

Accept responsibility to outline a master plan for the children.

Survey parents, teachers, and workers about programming, scheduling, and working together.

Utilize attendance figures and attitudes to determine the strength of current strategy and schedules.

3. COMMUNITY

An individual needs to belong, to be something and to do something. He wants to be accepted by other members of the church. He wants to feel at ease. When a person leaves a church you often hear: "I really never got connected," "I just couldn't find a place to fit in," or "It seemed that church members were not interested in forming relationships." Growing churches emphasize friendliness, forming friendships and being a friend.

A closer look—Three steps to action

Accept the fact that love, acceptance and forgiveness are required for a strong, thriving church.

Survey the attitudes of church members, greeters, ushers and those involved in assimilating members in the church.

Utilize a comprehensive tracking program for every visitor, regular attender and church member.

4. CONVENIENCE

We live in a "serve me" society. The church is not excluded from this prevailing sentiment. Four things impinge on church loyalty: location, traffic control, parking and time of activities. Convenience can result in greater commitment. Some move to another church because it is closer to home. This is legitimate because it provides more family time, reduces car expenses and permits more involvement in church activities. Traffic control and parking can also affect church loyalty. Some churches have off-campus parking and use shuttles to transport the people. The time and length of the services and activities are key factors also.

A closer look—Three steps to action

Accept the time demands that people operate under today. Usually church members live in a 20-mile radius of the church. Driving time for a family is from 15 to 35 minutes. Attending church on Sunday morning can require three to four hours, plus pre- and post-service responsibilities (dressing children, breakfast, personal grooming and lunch preparation). For mothers, this requires about eight hours.

Survey traveling distance by church members. Upgrade traffic control and parking ease. Plan service times and activities wisely and make meetings and events convenient to attend.

Utilize a "time team" to study time demands on church members and outline ways the church can better use time to both accommodate and serve the local congregation.

5. CONTROVERSY

Many people leave a church as a result of disagreement. Controversy can stem from doctrinal division, moral failure on the part of a leader, and twisted communication about church standards, goals, and operational procedures. Controversy always hurts the cause of Christ, disfigures the image of the church, and places a fence around the local harvest fields. Controversy cannot have a place in the body of Christ.

A closer look—Three steps to action

Accept the role of peacemaker, and you will be blessed. Always be positive. Constantly affirm, "God's will for our church is peace, unity and harmony. Together, let's claim it, practice it and enjoy it."

Survey the atmosphere of the church. Catch controversy before it erupts and spreads. Defuse with love, kindness and understanding.

Utilize different forms of promotion to build church unity — mission statement, membership classes, declarations by leaders and a motto such as, "At our church we believe in each other. Love binds us together and Christ beautifies us with His spirit."

6. CURRENCY

You have heard the statements: "All they talk about is money," "I don't want to give my money to build buildings, I want to help people," or "Why don't they talk more about love?" Some people don't want to embrace God's 10 percent tithing plan. And some do not want to support a building program. Others think giving money is a private matter and should be determined on an individual basis. Still others don't agree with the church budget. When their philosophy of giving or spending money is crossed, they leave the church.

A Closer Look—Three Steps to Action

Accept the fact that some people have not been taught to tithe. Help shape their stewardship awareness by your example and faith-building illustrations of God's financial plan for His church.

Survey the per capita giving of church members. This will reveal if there is a weakness in the teaching and training programs of the church.

Utilize a systematic plan of preaching, teaching, and training on financial stewardship and God's emphasis on sowing and reaping. Feature testimonies from faithful tithers and victory reports about overcoming debt and accepting God's methods of earning and spending money.

7. COMMITMENT

People do not support a person or a cause if they are not committed. Some individuals want spiritual rewards without accepting spiritual responsibilities. When they are challenged, conviction sets in and they leave. Also, some members are more committed than the church wants them to be. When there is both an awakening to worship in spirit and truth and to passionately win the lost, they leave.

A Closer Look — Three Steps to Action

Accept God's will that church members be committed. There comes a time that a decision must be made by each individual.

Survey the people involved in the ministry programs of the church. Are spiritual gifts being developed among the people? Is the church raising up leaders?

Utilize various methods to motivate people to a committed life. Commitment enables a believer to advance in Christian maturity, resulting in loyalty to the church, love for the unconverted and longsuffering toward other believers. Arrange for study programs—*Experiencing God*, *Authentic Worship*, and *Spirit-Powered Living*.

This resource section began with the words "Look closely at your church. People do leave." Then the question "Why?" was set forth. We have answered "why." We have listed *Steps to Action*. Now it is time to act! May you be blessed and your church elevated to a new height of health as you embrace the principles set forth and take positive steps of action.

Creating an Inviting Church Image

What is the attitude of people in the community and city toward your church? Is it favorable? Or is it tainted by frequent pastoral changes, church squabbles or undisciplined members? How people view the church is important for two reasons: 1) It reflects how they perceive the nature and work of God. 2) It either opens or closes the door to reaching the unchurched with the love of Christ. People generally hold one of six primary opinions or attitudes toward a local church. Three are negative and three are positive.

NEGATIVE OPINIONS

1. Unfriendly. This church builds a wall around it to protect it from worldly contamination. The people live to themselves and stay among themselves; they do not associate or build relationships with the unconverted. The community identifies the church with certain families or a "preacher." You hear comments like, "That's a close-knit church. I think they are satisfied with the group they have," or "I don't ever hear anything out of them. They don't participate in community or civic activities," or "I know two or three of their members but they don't ever mention their faith or the ministry of their church."

2. Unfaithful. "They don't live the love they talk about." Why would people make such a statement? Could their stance be legitimate? You can form your own conclusions as we examine some of the reasons:

- Constant pastoral changes. The Pastor, staff member, or prominent leader experienced a moral failure.
- Financial difficulties with the church making mortgage payments or being delinquent in paying bills.
- Church conflict, dividing into groups over a project or activity.
- Questionable reputation of a key church member in the city.
- Isolation where a church does not stand for or against moral issues, benevolence projects, improvements or social concerns.
- Inconsistencies in building a solid foundation of discipleship training and service to others.

3. Unorthodox. Core beliefs founded on God's Word must be embraced by a church for it to represent Christ authentically. Unorthodox means radical, uncommon, independent. Fad teachings, far-out interpretations of Scriptural promises or prophecies, or unfounded, faith-testing experiences in the history of the church paint a negative picture in the minds of individuals, even when the practices are not true or do not exist anymore. Perception becomes fact to them.

When people view a church as unorthodox, you hear statements such as, "I remember going to that church as a teenager. They did some bizarre things," "My grandmother went to that church, and I never understood some of the restrictive things she practiced," and "I know people who attend that church, and they have a long list of 'don'ts' and a short list of 'do's'." Negative opinions are difficult to erase.

POSITIVE OPINIONS

1. Friendly. This church is open, inviting and a part of the fabric of the city. They are a compassionate, caring and loving group of believers. Members build relationships with other churches, schools and civic groups. Comments: "You can always depend on that church; they care about the community," or "All I hear about that church is good. They look after their own, feed the hungry and provide for the needy," or "Church members share with me about the various ministries their church provides."

2. Faithful. "Those people practice what they profess." People make a statement such as this because of visible examples of Christian commitment and love. The walk of church members consists of both "faith" and "works." Look at some of the reasons people view a local church as faithful:

- Stability and integrity in tenure and performance of pastors, staff members and prominent leaders.

- Financial soundness—the church manages money wisely and maintains buildings and grounds with pride.

- Harmony, unity and close fellowship are evident. Conflict is resolved Scripturally and with sensitivity.

- Key church leaders are known in the city for their lifestyle of dedication to Christ and devotion to the church.

♦ Inside and outside the walls of the church there is involvement —social interaction, service projects and civic leadership. The church takes a stand on issues of moral purity and religious freedom.

♦ Christian maturity comes by focusing on daily devotions, prayer, and ministry to those dealing with perplexing situations.

3. Orthodox. Orthodox means following established doctrine— authoritative, official, approved. The Declaration of Faith serves as a true Biblical guide to keep the church in the center of God's plan. Christ is exalted, believers are equipped and the community is evangelized effectively. A local church with a history of sound doctrinal practices creates a positive image in the minds of people.

You hear statements that strengthen the congregation's image when the church is viewed as orthodox: "Those are good people at that church; they are an asset to our city," "The people at that church know what they believe and you can tell it by their behavior," and "I know a lot of people who attend that church. They are solid citizens and solid Christians. My relationship with them has made a difference in my life."

People will judge your church by what they see in your life.

Five Ways to Personally Strengthen the Image of Your Church

Show respect for the position of your Pastor. Embrace him as God's man leading the church to fulfill His will and timing.

Show authentic Christian commitment in the way you conduct business, relate to neighbors, and guide your children.

Show that you are a fully surrendered steward by your faithful giving to the church, in keeping your finances in order, and the way you view and value money.

Show respect for other churches and believers by sharing with them, praying for them, and working with them.

Show genuine concern for the unchurched and poverty-stricken by expressing love, offering guidance and providing assistance.

Five Ways a Church Can Strengthen Its Image

Join other churches in sponsoring citywide events—Thanksgiving service, civic projects, educational programs and care for the poor.

Promote ministries that touch the community and that build respect and trust for the church.

Maintain church property in such a way that it denotes pride and a commitment to quality. A "windshield tour" by neighbors can create a spirit of friendliness and welcome.

Maintain attractive signage and advertise the church. Place direction signs at strategic locations, feature ads in the local newspaper, and periodically do a citywide mailing.

Sponsor big events that gain the attention and the attendance of people from different areas of the city—seasonal plays, singing groups, crusades, special speakers, school projects (homework helpers), food functions and honor programs for public servants.

Small Things That Make a Church Big

We serve a big God, and bigness is a vital aspect of fulfilling the Great Commandment and the Great Commission. Bigness can represent spiritual maturity, numerical increases or a wide range of discipleship programs. A basic meaning of bigness, however, is "a dream and a driving commitment to reach the church's full potential in light of God's will, opportunities and talents."

A lot of small things lead to large things. Some big things must be done, too; they cannot be overlooked. In this lesson we will focus on three small things that make a church big.

EXUBERANT HOSPITALITY

We live in an impersonal world. People are lonely, seeking and longing for something they cannot identify. They look for a friendly church where they can make friends. They want to be loved, affirmed and accepted. Exuberant hospitality is the initial step in meeting this challenge.

Hospitality begins with eye contact; big, broad smiles; and handshakes that convey a feeling of, "You are welcome. We're glad you're here!" This must be taught and practiced until it becomes natural throughout the congregation.

Greeters must bubble with enthusiasm.

Ushers must unite with greeters to build an atmosphere of "You are important" and "We want to serve you."

Trained workers should man the Welcome Center to distribute colorful, informational brochures that describe church ministries.

Hospitality holds the doors to the church open so people will come in. On the other hand, hospitality closes the back doors of the church so people will stay and become members of the church family.

Following these principles takes the cooperation of all the body.

EXPRESSIVE LOVE

Love is the Bible's central theme. This theme is emphasized by the actions of the Triune God: Father, Son and Holy Spirit.

♦ God so loves—He gave His Son.

♦ Christ so loves—He submitted to the cross.

♦ The Holy Spirit so loves—He equips believers.

Members who love one another and the unchurched reflect the true nature of Christ. They identify with God.

We must express love in order to be effective and impact lives. This is Biblical and mandatory. People are attracted to a love-based church. When love is genuine and it is expressed, people will attend and they will bring others with them.

Love is expressed in many ways. First, it is an attitude. It says in words and actions, "We care about you as a person—your needs, goals and personal happiness."

Follow-up with guests who attend your church. You can do this with letters, visits, phone calls, and by tracking the newcomers' attendance and involvement. This includes providing members with a feeling of belonging, importance and significance. It includes all the qualities of 1 Corinthians 13.

Little expressions of love make a big impact on the community—things like food, clothing and assistance programs for the needy.

A church will be known by how it expresses love. Love beautifies people, liquidates problems and multiplies opportunities.

EXCITING ACTIVITIES

Church should be a happy, fun place! Church should be the source of luster and glow in life. Dull churches have small, dwindling attendance. Growing churches have exciting, uplifting activities.

Our fast-paced society and the advance of technology has created in all of us a very short attention span. This impacts how we conduct church and the activities we offer.

Programs must be life-related and well-planned. They must offer something that provides personal meaning.

Exciting activities attract attention in the community and denote freshness in the church. A big activity should be sponsored at least once a quarter: Christmas, Easter, Back-to-School, Fall Festival. This maintains anticipation among church members and creates interest in the community.

A major aspect of excitement is promotion. A church must constantly promote in order to attract attention and establish an identity of a visionary, progressive church.

All forms of promotion should be utilized: signs, newspaper ads, church bulletin, radio/television, billboards, flyers, direct mail, telephone calls, doorknob hangers and imprinted items.

Doing little things and doing them consistently can make a big difference in your church. They must be practiced because they are right, because they are easy to do and because that will help you and your church fulfill your ministry.

"Who has despised the day of small things?" (Zechariah 4:10). Certainly not the growing church and certainly not the big church. Details are so important.

Remember: little things make a church big!

How to BLESS Your Pastor

B — BOLDLY Stand With Him

Get on board the Old Ship of Zion, the local church, and stand with your Pastor. Make it a heart decision. Say, "I know my Pastor is chosen by God, called and commissioned to be a shepherd and servant-leader, and I will stand with him, boldly, faithfully, trustworthily."

L — LEARN to Love Him

Love is a decision. Your Pastor has a physical personality and a spiritual personality. Both of these reflect the way he relates, responds, and represents the local church. You learn to love him by showing respect for him as a person, as your Pastor, and the methods by which he fulfills the Great Commission.

E — ENJOY His Leadership

"Following the leader" can be fun, exciting and personally beneficial; it doesn't have to be boring. Pray, "Father, let me see Your hand of direction in my Pastor's leadership, and let me experience Your joy as I follow him . . . as he follows You."

S — SERVE With Him

Understand that you are not serving the Pastor *for* the Lord— you are serving *with* him. It is a partnership role. You work hand-in-hand, side-by-side, faith-with-faith to perform God's will for the local church and to advance His Kingdom universally—"we're together in mission."

S — SHOUT Victory With Him

We are laborers together, co-workers; we share in the fruit of the harvest. When victories are achieved, it is the result of teamwork. The people and the Pastor rejoice together as a team, a family and as God's people doing His work.

How to Be SALT for Your Pastor

Be SENSITIVE to his Needs—All of Them.
Recognize the Pastor's humanity; don't put all his needs in a spiritual box. He wrestles with some of the same issues that you do—eliminating tension in marriage, disciplining children, stretching the budget, feeling accepted and appreciated, and fulfilling his purpose in life.

Be ALERT to God's Plan—His Total Plan.
God's plan for the church is three-pronged: Enrichment (worship), Education (discipleship) and Evangelism (outreach). Balance and harmony are stabilized when attention is given to each area. You understand your Pastor's actions better when you understand God's plan.

Be LOVING in Relationships—Honest and Transparent.
Love God, love others, love yourself; that's the Biblical pattern. This approach is based on openness and togetherness—*worshipping* together, *working* together, and achieving *wholeness* together. Build a relationship with your Pastor founded on the true you.

Be TRUSTWORTHY in Mission—Fully Engaged.
God wants you to be successful in church ministry. That's why he gives spiritual gifts. Your Pastor is able to major on his assignments and the church is able to function as a coordinated body when you *discover* your spiritual gift, *develop* it, and *deploy* it in ministry.

How to Form a Spiritual "Trust Fund" With Your Pastor

A "trust fund" is something you can depend on and build your life around. This is true both financially and spiritually.

We are told in the Bible to trust in the Lord with all our heart (our energy and emotions) and not depend on our own knowledge (our skills and abilities). By following this pattern we are promised that God will direct our path and make it smooth and straight (see Proverbs 3:5, 6). This establishes a trust fund with God. What a powerful promise! Building a "trust fund" with God involves three faith-based steps:

♦ Look to Him in all things and for all things.

♦ Lean on Him for support and encouragement.

♦ Learn from His Word the patterns He uses to give grace, to guide, and to bestow gifts. This "trust fund" with God is always available and adequate—ready and sufficient.

A "trust fund" should be established with your Pastor. This "trust fund," like the one with your heavenly Father, involves three action steps:

♦ Look to your Pastor as God-appointed, and as a partner with you in doing the work of the church.

♦ Lean on your Pastor in love, and depend on him for Scriptural indoctrination and spiritual motivation.

♦ Learn your Pastor's personal make-up and ministry style—leadership characteristics, how he develops relationships, and his vision and concern for discipleship training and evangelistic outreach.

Your "trust fund" with your Pastor will honor his position, equip you for effective ministry, and bring both of you together as a happy team serving God according to His divine design.

How to Adopt a Share Plan With Your Pastor

The word *share* has many shades of meaning. They include giving and receiving, going and coming, laughing and crying, abundance and scarcity, highs and lows, successes and setbacks, answering and telling, triumphs and problems. All of these things surface when considering a "share plan" with your Pastor.

As we look at the "share plan," eight areas will be set forth:

♦ Share vision and the *demands* of vision.

♦ Share worship and the *commitments* of worship.

- Share discipleship and the *lifestyle* of discipleship.
- Share finances and the *inconveniences* of finances.
- Share blessings and the *responsibilities* of blessings.
- Share relationships and the *perplexities* of relationships.
- Share evangelism and the *anxieties* of evangelism.
- Share revival and the *sacrifices* of revival.

How to Love Your Pastor

- Love him with unconditional love, and affirm his ministry.
- Love him with obedient love, and follow his leadership.
- Love him with responsive love, and perform service.
- Love him with witnessing love, and spread the good news.
- Love him with praying love, and intercede for him.
- Love him with believing love, and back him with faith.
- Love him with giving love, and support him financially.
- Love him with grateful love, and honor him.
- Love him with loyal love, and stand firmly with him.
- Love him with bold love, and promote his vision.

How to Invest in Your Pastor's Ministry

When you invest there will be positive returns. This is both sound and Scriptural. It is part of God's law of sowing and reaping. This is the path for church balance, church health and church growth. Let's consider some ways you can invest in your Pastor's ministry:

Prayer. Pray for your Pastor every day. Offer petitions for his effectiveness in leading, preaching and nurturing.

Promotion. Promote the ministry of your Pastor. Encourage the congregation to trust him, follow him and back him.

Participation. Participate in programs that foster love for the Pastor. Emphasize lifting him up and positioning him for victory.

Partnership. Partner with your Pastor in ministry. View yourself as a co-worker, fulfilling God's divine design for the local church.

Prosperity. Champion prosperity for your Pastor. Stress the importance of adequate salary structure as well as acts of appreciation.

How to Feel What Your Pastor Feels

♦ **Understand his calling.** The Pastor's call from God (Ephesians 4:11) can never be withdrawn (Romans 11:29).

♦ **Embrace his compassion.** The Pastor observes the model of Christ; he weeps over the city and the welfare of the people (Luke 19:41).

♦ **Join his commission.** "Preach Good News to the poor . . . heal the brokenhearted . . . announce that captives shall be released . . . and the blind shall see . . . the downtrodden shall be freed . . . and that God is ready to give blessings to all who come to Him" (Luke 4:18, 19, *TLB*).

The Good Shepherd Pastor

In John 10:11 Christ said, "I am the good shepherd. The good shepherd gives His life for the sheep." Christ set the example for being a good shepherd. Look at three ways He gave His life:

1. He gave up His **divine life** in heaven with God the Father and the heavenly host to come to earth;

2. He gave up His **physical life** on earth to minister, and to pay the price for salvation;

3. He gave His up **relational life** on earth with His disciples and followers to return to heaven to represent all the people at the right hand of God the Father.

Christ is the Chief Shepherd (1 Peter 5:4), but He has selected Pastors to be shepherds under His appointment: "Then I will give you shepherds (Pastors) after my own heart, who will lead you with knowledge and understanding" (Jeremiah 3:15, *NIV*).

His admonition to them is "shepherd the flock of God" (1 Peter 5:2), and "shepherd the church of God" (Acts 20:28). To follow the pattern of the Great Shepherd, Jesus Christ, a Pastor must give his life for the sheep.

How does a Pastor give his life for his sheep? He must follow the path Christ took. Three things in the life of Christ relate to the life of your Pastor:

1. He must give his **spiritual life** to the Father in order to connect with people and lead them in the ways of God.

2. He must give his **physical life** to prayer, study, visiting and paying the price for church health and maturity.

3. He must give his **relational life** to live among the people and to lead, feed and defend them.

As a Good Shepherd Pastor, a Pastor's life is not his own. He is "souled-out." He is totally committed to God's call on his life—to represent Him to the people.

Powerful Ideas
How to Keep Close to Your Pastor and Foster Church Health

—God's Plan—

It is God's plan for the Pastor and people to stay close together, as partners, friends and co-workers, in serving Him and performing Kingdom ministry. These 29 powerful ideas provide us clear directions in order to "move mountains" and to be "motivated for ministry."

1. **PUBLICIZE** the positive and give exceptional service to the church. This will create an environment of faith, expectation, and spiritual self-worth.

2. **UNDERSTAND** the value of church members and the negative impact when just one is lost. This will stimulate watchfulness and emphasize love and protective care for each other.

3. **CHERISH** the talents and contribution of every member. This builds loyalty and increases harmonious relationships.

4. **STUDY** the different spiritual zones church members are in—Dissatisfied, Satisfied, Spiritually Motivated. This will assist in making plans to recruit, revive, and re-direct.

5. **DISPLAY** a spirit of expectation and excitement. It will affect others, and ministry momentum will be increased.

6. **GREET** members and visitors promptly and sincerely. This conveys acceptance, shows that your church is a friendly place and contributes to building relationships.

7. **ANTICIPATE** needs of the church, volunteer workers and your Pastor. This positions you to lead and to help build faith to move with God.

8. **COMPLIMENT** freely and sincerely. This marks you as one who understands the functions of the church as a body with its varied and valuable members.

9. **SOLICIT** negative feedback about church programs and activity. This positions the church to avoid stagnation and to improve continually.

10. **GUARD** your timing on follow-up requests by prompt action and accountability. This shows true concern, trustworthiness and dependability.

11. **EXPLAIN** the policies of the church and the reason things are done in a certain way. This prevents misunderstandings.

12. **EXERCISE** caution when extolling the values of your church. Don't under-promise or over-deliver. This shows you are trying to help people and not just increase church attendance.

13. **SHOW** attention to unhappy or irate church members. Treat them with respect by listening to them and by handling their problems quickly. This erects a bridge of acceptance and satisfaction.

14. **DISARM** chronic complainers with faith, facts and friendship. This forces them to propose solutions to problems.

15. **UTILIZE** the E-plus Factor—exceed the expectations of friends and visitors by going the second mile. This creates excitement, clarifies vision and establishes confidence.

16. **CREATE** a climate of caring by showing genuine attention. Always, absolutely, positively care! This reveals true Christlike and Scriptural love.

17. **HELP** reward workers for faithful actions and performance. This establishes trust, cooperation and "happy" volunteers.

18. **PARTICIPATE** in training and building committed and competent church members. This gives them a sense of contribution and readiness for caring for the flock and reaping the harvest.

19. **RESCUE** your Pastor from unreasonable requests by demonstrating insight on the many demands for his time. This strengthens him and fosters a greater spirit of working with him.

20. **GIVE** your Pastor a break from the multitude of ongoing demands on his time, emotions, energy and family. This enables him to stay sharp, and do his work with both freshness and intensity.

21. **NURTURE** a partnership in ministry with your Pastor. This will set in motion a bonding process and establish a set of values that will guide harmony and togetherness in fulfilling God's will.

22. **RECOGNIZE** and reinforce what is being done right in the church. This adds value to the church mission and to those performing at a high level of spiritual commitment.

23. **PROMOTE** the benefits of church membership and the spiritual rewards of church loyalty. This results in happier church members and provides greater opportunities to care and nurture.

24. **MAINTAIN** a positive attitude about the decisions of the Pastor and the direction he takes. This opens doors of understanding and demonstrates Biblical trust.

25. **LEARN** to translate Scriptural injunctions into daily be-havior (Matthew 7: 12). This shows authentic Christian commitment and builds a platform from which to witness.

26. **PRACTICE** adding value to your Pastor's sermons by applying them, complimenting him and sharing them with others. This shows Christian character and challenges oth-ers to think and act on Scriptural truth.

27. **CONTRIBUTE** to creating an environment of intimacy with God through worship that always exalts Him. This depicts your church as a true place to meet and know God.

28. **ENCOURAGE** friends and neighbors to attend church functions with you. As you build relationships with them, it shows you sincerely care about them as individuals.

29. **EXPECT** to experience God every time you attend church by preparing for worship. This impacts your life, the life of your Pastor and the lives of other attendees.

How to Be a True Friend to Your Pastor

F — Be **Faithful** in church attendance.

R — Be **Respectful** of his responsibilities.

I — Be **Informed** about church goals.

E — Be **Excited** in worship services.

N — Be **Nurtured** by fellowship with him.

D — Be **Dedicated** to supporting him.

The Pastor – My True Friend

1. I will *confide* in him.

2. I will *see* his point of view.

3. I will *make plans* with him.

4. I will *have fun* with him.

5. I will *show* respect for him.

6. I will *trust* his decisions.
7. I will *labor* faithfully with him.

The Pastor and You

I saw a loving pastor,
 visionary,
 committed and meek.
But he was stretched in his work,
 pushed,
 pressed, and
 had little rest.
I became confused and said,
 "God, this is not right.
 Why don't you act and
 correct the plight?"
There was silence.
 I waited,
 reflected with a
 sense of personal protest.
Then God suddenly said,
 "I know the plight.
 I have acted to make it right;
 I created you!"

How to Be a Comfort to Your Pastor

In his closing remarks in the letter to the Colossians, Paul lists the names of individuals he referred to as "fellow workers for the kingdom" who had been "a comfort" to him (4:11). A Pastor needs people who "comfort him"—provide sustaining strength, Scriptural support and spiritual encouragement.

What distinguished the five individuals Paul listed—Tychicus, Onesimus, Aristarchus, Mark, and Justus—from all the other people? One trait: they "proved to be a comfort to [him]."

What did they do? As we look at each individual, observe the qualities and actions that will "prove to be a comfort" to your Pastor and embrace them.

1.   **Tychicus** – his name means **fortunate**. He was blessed, successful, happy, prosperous, bright and outgoing in his personality. He was a messenger for Paul. He took Paul's letters to the Ephesians and Colossians, and read them to the churches. Tychicus was a great **comfort** to Pastor Paul because he could be depended on to fulfill an assignment with dignity, dedication and excellence.

2.   **Onesimus** – his name means **profitable**. He was the slave of Paul's convert, Philemon. He was converted under Paul's ministry at Rome, and traveled with Tychicus to carry letters to the Colossians and to his owner, Philemon. He was willing to pay the price of discipleship and go back to Philemon from whom he had run away.

Paul said to Philemon that Onesimus "is profitable to you and to me" (Philemon 11), so receive him as a "beloved brother" (v. 16). **Onesimus** brought Pastor Paul **comfort** because of his willing attitude to mend broken relationships and to pay the price to minister.

3.   **Aristarchus** – his name means **the best ruler.** Paul spoke of him as a fellow-prisoner, implying imprisonment for the Gospel's sake. He stayed by Paul in the good times, the bad times and the hard times. **Aristarchus** brought **comfort** to Pastor Paul because he was always there—never shirking his duty, but steadfast and solid in faith and friendship.

4.   **Mark** – his name means a large **hammer.** Mark was a personal attendant of Paul and Barnabas when they set out on their great mission tour (Acts 13:5). He failed them in a crisis but recovered and became a valued colleague of Paul (Colossians 4:10, 11). **Mark** brought Pastor Paul **comfort** because he would not let failure be final. He became a **helper of others**; he served others.

5.   **Justus** – his name means **just** or **righteous.** He was included in the salutation to the Colossian church because he knew how to treat his Pastor. **Justus** brought Paul **comfort** because he

treated him with honor, provided basic needs, and made sure he was comfortable and secure.

You can be a **comfort** to Your Pastor by demonstrating the characteristics of the five men who assisted Pastor Paul. Review them, develop them, and then let them be evident in your relationship with your Pastor.